THE SQUARE HEAP

THE SQUARE HEAP

BY DORA LEE MCKEE

Surrogate Press®

Published in the United States by
Surrogate Press®
an imprint of Faceted Press®
Surrogate Press, LLC
Park City, Utah

SurrogatePress.com

ISBN: 978-1-964245-24-9

Library of Congress Control Number: 2025920560

Book Cover design by: Michelle Rayner, Cosmic Design
Interior design by: Katie Mullaly, Surrogate Press®

In loving memory.

Chapter One

It wasn't square. Nor it wasn't really a heap neither, strictly speaking. It was the way he said it. Not like he was sorry about it, nor ashamed. Just said it plain out, like he didn't care what I'd make of it. It was just there and that was a flat fact.

"It's just a heap." He eyed it appraisingly, "Kinda square. Reckon it's a square heap, you might say."

It didn't have a name, and if it had, it likely would not have been called that, but always, all the rest of my life, I thought of it like that. Truly, it was not heaped nor square either, but mounded gentle and soft at the corners. It had good cause to be so, for the space between the straight log walls on the inside and the queer outside walls was packed tightly with clay hauled from the river banks. A good weather-tight house, all in all. Warm in the wintertime and cool in the summertime.

Its roof was thatched and more clay packed atop that. I'd never seen anything like it, nor not apt to neither. And I never did. It was a one of a kind, it was the Square Heap.

The door was low. He had to stoop more than a little to go in. I clutched my shawl tightly and took a deep breath before I followed. I was set on seeing as much as I could on that first look around.

Muslin, dyed black, was tacked over the holes cut for windows. In the far wall was a big stone hearth, and it had a good blazing fire. The floor was the same sod we'd just stepped off of, but harder packed, and it showed marks of a twig broom. Inside you could tell it wasn't square. No one wall matched another for size.

They were there too! I tried not to stare. His advertisement had plainly said "with family." There was a sharp lurch in the middle of my chest, but it settled down right quick. No pain to me that he already had young'uns.

I didn't expect love. I expected to be of use. And from what I had seen, there was no gainsaying that there was sure plenty of use for me here.

I usually don't get tired too easy but the trip was long, and being wed to a stranger did upset me a mite. I have to say I was tired then. It didn't matter. I took off my best shawl and my bonnet and pushed up my sleeves. He dropped my carpet bag on the bed, hunched his big shoulders in his shabby coat, and stamped out again. I heard the leather creaking, the jingling of tack, the crack and turn of the wagon wheels.

My new shoes had pinched my feet for nearly the whole trip so I hurried, glad that I'd had the foresight to tuck my old ones into the carpet bag. There was a clean apron there too, and I tied it on. I would have liked to have my stays off, but those big eyes watched without a blink.

The sideboard was just exactly high enough so that I knew I was in for an eternal backache. Humph! *She* must have been one of those little ones! And not overly strong neither. Even without fetching the lamp, the crisscross knife marks, black with ground in dirt, stood out on the cloudy yellow of the planking. Nothing I cooked would touch that table until it had a proper good scrubbing.

I pushed the slat board door, with no latch or handle, and carrying the lamp from the big eating table, I found the pantry and lifted up the light. I "humphed" again. Lazy too, likely! The shelves were nearly bare! And the rafters too! The potatoes, what few there were left, were shriveled and beginning to sprout. There was a partial sack of meal and a little lard in the can. Out of sorts with any woman that would let her larder get in such shape, I took the lone ham from the rafter, tucked the meal and the lard can under my arm, and pushed my way through the door.

"You ain't gonna cut the ham!" the boy gasped.

"Am," I thunked it down heavily on the dirty sideboard.

"Pa won't like it!" he threatened.

"Uh-huh," I grunted, and finding a great knife, I sunk it sure and clean to the bone and circled it round directly in the middle of the ham.

The boy's mouth gaped open in horror.

"I gots grits in the pot," the girl almost whispered.

I looked at her squarely. Her eyes were like violets, so blue they were, mighty near purple, and they were as big as saucers with awe as she stared up at me. Her look slewed sidewise to her brother, then down. Her little face was pinched and pale, her twisting hands awfully tiny and thin.

I put my chin over my shoulder to look at the hearth and went back to slicing ham.

"Do you always put the pot in the ashes?" I demanded.

"Jim Beam wouldn't lift it for me," her answer was hold-offish. The boy glared at her.

I grunted again and went to reach the pot out onto the hearth. I used a corner of my apron to lift the heavy lid. Yeah, there were grits in the pot. A cup, or might be two, in the bottom. On top of them was half a gallon of water, far from boiling, with little circles of fat from the lard she had added for flavor. Not fit for the hogs! I replaced the lid and pushed it aside. I went back to slicing ham. If Jim Beam's eyes kept on getting bigger, they'd pop!

"Do we have a baking board?" I asked the girl.

She skittered off and back, holding it up for me. I sighed impatiently. It was hardly cleaner than the sideboard. But I reckoned if they'd been eating the dirt anyhow, it wouldn't do them no more harm one last time, and there wasn't no time for scouring now.

Jim Beam goggled and declared constantly that, "Pa won't like it!" The little girl watched in awe while I mixed the pone and greased the board. It wouldn't be like skillet bread, of course, with milk and eggs, but it would be bread, and dipped in the red ham drippings likely to be tolerable tasty!

I had to dig into the shallow shelves under the sideboard for salt. That seemed to be what we had the most of. I found some sugar. And in a small tin box, a treasure! Two table-spoonfuls of tea!

I shook my head at the grimy water pail and the rag stopped dipper. The tinker would get that first time around! I ladled water into the heavy teakettle and hung it on the crane. I stirred the fire beneath it and put on a bit more wood. I set the baking board where the heat would be right, wedged the spider forward with the toe of my shoe, and set a huge skillet of ham to frying. I greased the pick of the pota-toes, rolled them in cold ashes, and buried them in the pop-ping coals with a stick of kindling wood.

In the shelves under the sideboard were such utensils as we had and I busied myself setting the table. The girl sat back on her heels and stared at the cooking food like she was spellbound.

Jim Beam, overtaken with the notion that I had done all this that "Pa wouldn't like" shot his last bolt. "Can't use the lamp!" he shouted. "It's our only one and we ain't got no more coal oil."

I blew out the lamp. "We got candles?" I asked him.

"Naw!" he shouted, but the girl sprang up away from him and ran to fetch several small stumps.

I placed them side by side in an extra tin plate and left them to be lighted when the man came in. He was taking an uncommon long time in caring for the horse.

I turned the ham. Its sweet smell swelled out into the room and there was the tantalizing odor of the singeing potato peels. The lard on the bread board sizzled and sputtered about the browning edges of the bread. The little girl sat with her hands clasped limply in her lap, her eyes half closed, the only thing about her alive was her twitching little nose. Even Jim Beam, having done his best, gave up and sat in open-eyed, slack-jawed silence.

I heard the stump of his boots. He thrust the door inward and halted. I turned away for a blazing splinter to light the candle stubs. I lit them and still he stood. He shouldered my small trunk, but he seemed to have forgotten it.

The girl turned her face, the dancing yellow-orange flames behind her head lent her features a delicate, fey quality, and fear wrenched sharply at my heart. The man jerked, moved sharply, and that unholy charge was gone, but I knew he had felt it too. I touched the shaggy, dirt-matted mop of her hair as I went to retrieve the baking board and its bread.

"Come to the table, Jim Beam!" I ordered sharply.

Jim Beam, sparked by my manner, leapt, not to obey, but to take his stool, the easier to tattle. He ran down all my failings loudly and it took him several breaths since he made as much as any wild imagination could out of my simple acts. I didn't listen. I cut the bread and served it, leaving the board on the table. I dusted the potatoes and squeezed them open, tumbling out their mealy white insides. I served up the pink sizzling ham and spooned out its red juices.

Jim Beam was at last silent.

But before I steeped the tea, or sat down to my own portion, I went to delve in my trunk. It was foolish, I know, but I gave away my only treasure. I dropped it over her head on my way to my chair.

The man's eyes hit me like a blow. I had done wrong. I could not help it.

Jim Beam had to round the table to take it in his hand. And the girl spooned her food into her mouth with one hand while she clutched the tiny golden locket in fingers as delicate as the trinket itself.

They ate as I had known they would, starved for good, decent, palatable, woman-cooked food. No wonder, if they were used to the half-raw, greasy, drowned, lukewarm grits. And yet, their mannerisms gave me an insight into the man I had married. They were proud. They ate slowly, savoring every bite, holding back their hunger. So I watched and replenished their plates as they wanted.

I didn't forget to blow out the candles as soon as the meal was done. The dishes were put by quickly, for I had the kettle boiling and the utensils were few.

The man drained the last of his sweet tea and put down his tin cup, "Beth!"

The girl dashed up, tidied the table, and dried and put away as I washed. The water bucket was nearly empty. I wiped out the dishpan.

"We need more water," I stated.

Beth caught the bail, but I stopped her with one hand.

"Jim Beam, you fetch in some water."

He started up, his food-drugged lids snapping wide over his eyes. "Pa!" he wailed.

His pa stared at him solidly. He gave in with small grace. He brought back half a bucketful. My husband sat, his heavy arms propped on the table and he gazed into the fire.

I dug again into my trunk and I used the bend of my head to hide my wry smile. Gramma Hildebrand knew a lot, but she didn't know it all. I touched and grasped my needles and a hank of the fine yarn. I sat down on a low stool near the fire for light. Beth, who had followed me with her eyes, crept near. I cast on for a sock. Surely, I didn't know his measurements, but if they were too small, Jim Beam would grow into them soon.

"I know a story," I knit and purled and waited.

"Tell it," she whispered at last.

I pulled my yarn loose and settled as best I could. My stays bound my full stomach uncomfortably.

"Well, once upon a time there was a stork," I began.

"A stork?" She seemed puzzled.

"A stork, dummy!" Jim Beam chortled and he leaped in a wild dance before me. "A stork! A big bird what brings babies!"

Beth gasped. I didn't miss a stitch.

"Well now," I went on easily, "all storks don't bring babies, Jim Beam. Happens this here stork didn't. No, sir!

Matter of fact, he didn't do much a-tall. And he had a friend. An awful funny friend. A fox!"

"A fox?" Jim Beam fell backwards, "Aw! Ain't so!"

"Of course, it's so. In this here story, it's so. Well like I say, they were friends, but not best friends mind. Of course, ol' Fox was sly and he was kinda mean too. Anyhow, one day he played a kind of mean joke on Stork. He asked Stork to his cave for supper. Now Stork didn't much wanna go, 'cause you see, he knew ol' Fox was a sly one. But Fox was his friend, so he went. Stork went and Fox was so polite and everything was just fine until Fox, he put the supper on."

"Ha!" shrieked Jim Beam, "I know it, I know it! Stork was the supper!" Beth's eyes flew wide in alarm. I tucked my lips.

"Well, not exactly, Jim Beam. The supper was soup. Just plain old soup. But you see, ol' Fox being mean like he was, just served it up in little shallow pans. And Fox, well he laps his all up and he laughs at Stork because everyone knows storks can't lap. Storks have got long beaks and can't drink out of shallow pans."

Jim Beam pounced at once, "So Stork was a fool for going!" he yelled. "That's a dumb story!"

I flashed amused eyes at Beth. She was quick as I had known she would be.

"No, he wasn't, Jim Beam!" she cried, "We ain't heard it all yet!"

"That's right," I nodded, "Stork wasn't so dumb. He says 'thankee' nicely to Fox and he asked Fox to come to his house for supper the next night. Now, you see, Jim Beam, Fox was the dumb one, because he says of course he'd go."

"He wasn't!" Jim Beam screamed, "'Cause Fox ate Stork!"

"Oh, no!" breathed Beth.

"Of course not!" I stated, and finished quickly, "Stork, he served soup too, only he served it up in pitchers. Pitchers with long necks. Stork, he ate his meal just fine, but Fox, he went away hungry!"

Beth stuffed her fingers into her mouth. She giggled around them. She chortled, she flung out her tiny hands and laughed aloud. She spun out onto the floor. "Oh, Jim Beam!" she laughed, "Oh, Jim Beam!"

His face went red. It contorted with rage. He leapt in front of her. "Dumbbell, Beth!" he shouted, "Stupid Beth!" and he punched forward with a knotted fist.

Her face went pale, she clutched her stomach and folded forwards. It didn't come to me to look to the man. I was too newly wed for that. I shot out my arm, I caught the boy, split his britches down the back seam, and I blistered his bare bottom.

I am not a puny woman. I stand as tall as most men. My shoulders are wide, my back strong, and I was never so grateful for the broad palms of my hands as I was then. Nor for my even temper.

I slammed the boy solidly down on his stool. "You will always respect your sister," I told him calmly. "You remember that."

"Aaah!" He was screeching at the top of his lungs, "My nose . . . gonna bleed!"

"Hmmm. You best to go bleed outside then, Jim Beam," and I bent to lift the gasping girl from the floor.

"Pa!"

I had forgotten the man altogether. Now it was almost funny to watch Jim Beam go clomping across the floor, one hand holding his torn breeches and red bottom, and the other cupped against his nose which for sure wasn't bleeding, to stand by his Pa.

I faced around on the man. Like as not he'd give me a trouncing to pay for the one I'd just handed out to his manchild. But he didn't. He didn't even look at Jim Beam. He slammed a great fist down on the table top and he laughed. A loud, roared, bitter laugh with nothing funny in it, and he turned and stamped out the door leaving us all to do as we would. It gave me a start, his being so plum disinterested. We didn't see him again the rest of the night.

Well, the upshot of it all was that Jim Beam's nose never did bleed, and Beth, after looking for a while like she was going to die, got her breath back and didn't come close to it. Didn't seem she weighed hardly more than the ham, and under the flimsy, floppy dress there sure wasn't much to her but bones.

"Where do you young'uns sleep?" I asked Jim Beam.

He was feeling mean and gave me a look like killing, but he was getting a little respect too, so he pointed up.

Between the corner that had the bed and the hearth there was a rickety, narrow ladder against the wall. On top of that, there was a narrow plank runway into the corner. Why it was no more than a cubbyhole under the eaves. Barely enough room for them to stretch out, but anyhow, it was warm.

I looked at him, "Do you want to go outdoors?"

He turned beet red and scuttled up the ladder. The plank bounced fearfully under his slamming feet.

"Throw down your britches," I called at him, "I've got to sew them up."

I was positive sure that he didn't have but the one pair, but I didn't ask him then. I reckoned Jim Beam's temper would settle when his bottom cooled off.

Beth patted me softly, "I reckon I've got to go," she whispered.

I knew that for what it was, so I got my shawl.

She skipped and danced in front of me, her dress blowing in the chill breeze. She had nothing about her save that dress and she was barefooted, so I tucked her up in my shawl and carried her back to the house.

I was never a queasy woman, but I couldn't watch her run across the plank. I got Jim Beam's britches from where he had thrown them on the bed, and got my sewing box, and used the last of the firelight to sew them up.

When I was sure they were asleep, I stood myself in the corner beneath their cubbyhole and made ready for bed. Once I laid down, I had to breathe deep a few times, it felt so good to be shunt of my stays. I reckoned I'd not wear them again unless it be to funerals and, mayhap, weddings, and to church, did I get the chance to go.

Chapter Two

I slept two rows at a time that night, for I don't believe I turned over once. I woke at dawn, because that was my habit. The bed beside me was empty and it had been all night. The bar to the door was where I had left it, still standing against the jamb.

I got dressed and spread up the bed. I picked up my new shoes and bent to place them underneath. They wouldn't go and I got down on my knees to find out why. I caught at the obstacle and tugged. It came out easy. A trundle bed! I pushed it back and got up. There was nothing peculiar, or even particular about a trundle bed. There was something peculiar about the young'uns not using it.

I kindled a fire, mixed mush, set it to boil, and hung the kettle on the crane. I made a trip out to the outhouse and I cleaned everything from the shelves under the sideboard and set it on top. Wedged away back in the corner I found another skillet. I set potatoes to frying and I cut more ham.

I found a tiny pot. I don't know what *she* used it for, but it was perfect for my purposes. I wiped it out, poured in a little hot water and stirred it full of sugar. I had to take a piece of kindling to rake out a few coals to balance it on. A little sweetening for the mush.

In the mess that I had taken from the shelves was a small poke of dried beans. Without a qualm, I emptied Beth's grits, saving the kernels themselves in case there were hogs or chickens. I rinsed out the big pot and, sorting the beans through my fingers, I put them to soak. Later, the ham bone and the slivery trimmings would go in. Dinner and at least a part of supper. I could make more pone and just maybe I could find some greens.

I put the ham to frying. It was broad daylight. The man would be stirring outdoors. He'd be ready to eat soon. Even as I thought it, I heard the sound, the thwacking of an axe against wood. I nodded. I'd be needing hot water a-plenty this day and he'd be coming with an armload of firewood.

There was a sound from the cubby. My hand went to my head. I hadn't done up my hair, just pinned it back. I tucked my wrapper a little tighter at my throat and looked up.

Beth poked her head over the edge, "I smell it! I smell it!" she hummed.

"Well, shake up Jim Beam, come on down here and set the table," I turned back to the hearth.

I heard her jawing at Jim Beam a little and then she was there.

"Have we got anything to wash with?" I asked.

"Got this," she flittered so fast I shook my head.

Well, what she held up didn't resemble a towel in any way and it was so grey I didn't know for sure just what it was, but I nodded solemnly. I poured a little hot and a little cold in the dishpan and held it down. She stopped dead still, the towel in one hand and stared up at me. She had not been taught to wash! I was sharply impatient and I don't know what softened my tone.

"You can't come to the table without washing up!"

She did her best, which wasn't very good, but I nodded at her anyhow. I threw the used water out the door. And while I was there, I looked to see. Sure enough, there, on pegs against the wall, hung a boiler and a wash tub. I thanked my lucky stars. That meant baths. It also meant a rub board somewheres about. All I had to do was find it.

There was the way solid chunk of the axe. He had set it in the standing stump. I poured more hot water and cooled it with cold from the bucket, swishing it with my fingers to make sure.

Jim Beam strutted up. He was in no way impaired from our set-to of the night before. His bottom did not sting. He dipped his hands in, the door opened and I slapped him sidewise. Looked like I had to teach that boy everything!

"Boys wash up after their Pas!" I told him, and I held the towel for the man. He knew how to wash. He soused his head good and scrubbed at his face. He pushed up his sleeves and rubbed the water high on his arms. I gave him the towel. Then I held down the pan for Jim Beam. I hate to say it, but Jim Beam was downright mean. He made faces at me behind his Pa's back. He wouldn't come on my say so. His Pa swung a hand. Jim Beam dibbled his fingers and swiped his eyes and mouth. He took the towel from his Pa and dared me with his eyes squinted.

If he was my boy, he wouldn't have gotten away with it. But then, that was up to his Pa. Jim Beam was awful proud and I think that is a fine thing for a boy, but I'd have turned his pride where it belonged, instead of upon himself.

Beth scurried quickly and I nodded at her when she was right. She was like a tiny animal, so grateful for any praise. Yeah, Beth I'd be able to manage; Jim Beam, I didn't know. Raised as I had been among a family of seven brothers and all nearly grown when I was still a little one, I didn't know much about growing up men. I knew about Beth. She was coming up to be a woman.

I had no worries there; I was a woman. But Jim Beam? He was different.

He pushed back his stool and looked at his Pa. "I'm goin', Pa."

The man nodded but didn't look up. I waited, but I didn't let Jim Beam get out that door. His Pa ate all that was put in front of him. That was good. Made a woman feel like cookin' to see a man eat like that. He sipped the last of his chicory and pushed back his chair. Without a word, he stumped out. Jim Beam made to follow. I caught him sharp.

"You come here and sit down, Jim Beam," I ordered, "I'm not through with you yet."

Jim Beam came to the table, but he didn't sit.

"Are you helping your Pa?" I finished my mush.

"Naw," he dared me.

"Are you going hunting?"

"Naw," he wasn't giving me an inch.

I looked at him kinda flat-like, "Well, I reckon we'll just go hunting for an hour or two. I'll show you how to set a rabbit snare."

Jim Beam bridled. "You don't need to show me nuthin'!" he shouted.

Now I'm not one to fiddle around. I let him have it full force, "You are going to do your share around here, Jim Beam. You aren't a baby any more. We need meat. Your Pa's busy, so that leaves just you. I don't reckon to starve on account of your ornery self! We're going hunting!"

He turned beet red. He made an awful face and he flung out his arms wildly, "Beth can't come!" he screamed.

I looked at him. Jim Beam needed this. "No, Beth can't come," I said quietly.

I left her with the cleaning up to do. She smiled at me, her lips curving slowly over her teeth, her eyes dew-drenched so that somehow she jerked a knot in my throat. It made me more stern with Jim Beam than I aimed to be. I had to stretch to reach the gun down from over the hearth.

"Bullets?"

"Naw!" he shook his head.

"Powder and lead?"

Jim Beam moved faster than I had thought he could. We pushed away a clear space on the table. There was not enough light. I ripped down the black muslin from the windows. I showed Jim Beam how to measure the powder. After the second time, he was better at it than I was, so I let him do it.

"You ever shoot this gun, Jim Beam?"

"Naw!"

"It's time you learned."

It was a hard two hours for me. Jim Beam was over anxious, but after a bit he got the heft of the gun and did real well. I showed him how to set a snare, but he didn't seem handy at that, so I set them myself.

We flushed a covey of birds and by luck or not, Jim Beam got two. He insisted on carrying them home. He didn't really want to go back, but I promised we'd come again. He sure took to that gun. And he was mighty proud of those two pheasants. I was in a hurry. I walked fast. Must be coming up past eight o'clock and nothing done yet. It would take me a month of Sundays to get the cleaning done and that house running right.

But I paused when I found the poke greens and swooped up my apron to pick into. Jim Beam flopped down, breathing hard. He'd been trotting to keep up with me, so I let him be. I picked carefully but quickly, and I had a good mess in practically no time. I nodded to myself. Lip-smacking these would be, though I couldn't imagine any of this family smacking their lips.

One thing they sure had was table manners.

Another thing they sure had was pride! Jim Beam's chest stuck out a mile and he strutted like a young cockerel when we crossed the yard. Beth was watching for us. She burst out of the door and ran shrieking toward us. Poor Jim Beam, his ego was punctured right off.

"Jim Beam!" Beth shrieked, "Ma!"

Well, that gave me a turn, but I was glad she had come to it so easy. I caught her with one hand. Her eyes were huge with excitement.

"You'll never guess!" She cried and I hastened my steps. Something had happened.

I pushed through the door first. Something surely had happened! Well, I couldn't say I hadn't been warned. His advertisement read *with family*. Nothing was ever said about how much *"family."* This one bore the stamp of him on his face. As like as two peas in a pod! Except this one was red! Well, not really. Sort of a golden-copper color and he stood barely a head taller than Jim Beam. I guess I stared open-mouthed. Beth held to my hand and danced up and down.

"Ma! It's Flying Cloud!" Bless Jim Beam!

He strutted past me and thrust his birds nearly under the nose of this new young'un. "See that?" he shouted, "Hey! I killed 'em myself! Two! Two of 'em! Hey, Fly! Two of 'em!"

But the taller lad stood silent and looked to me. "Is this the new mother?" he asked of Beth.

"Yeah, Fly!" she squealed, "Ma! Fly's come home!"

Yeah! Fly had come home, and I'd have to be as thick as mud not to see it.

"How do, Fly," I stood there holding the poke greens.

"Then, I am welcome?" His tone was solemn, his speech flawless, but there was something in his eyes.

"This is your Pa's home. It's yours, too." I dumped my poke greens on Beth's clean table.

Like it or not, that was the way it was. I took it in my stride. I put the gun back up over the hearth.

"Hang those birds in the pantry, Jim Beam. Then you and Fly go out and fetch me a couple of good strong straight sticks to roast them on." I looked down and Beth was just below my elbow. "Wait! Take the wash tub down. Put in a couple of buckets of water. Then fill the boiler. Then get the sticks."

They carried the tub between them nearly to the door. It was about half full. I dipped out a kettle full and set it to boil. I pushed the bean pot into the fire on the spider. The rest of the morning hours flew. I carried the wash tub inside the house and in front of the fire I scrubbed Beth to within an inch of her life, head and all. After that, she fetched me a miserable-looking thing that was their comb. It had lost more than half its teeth. I could never have got it through her long hair. I fetched my own comb and brush, and when I was through, I fetched a couple of wisps of red yarn to tie off her braids. I thought she looked beautiful, but Jim Beam— well, he was Jim Beam.

"Ha! You look like a skinned cat, Beth! Yaa! Yaa! Skinned cat, Beth!"

The soap was good strong lye soap and there was plenty of it. I used it. The side board was white and sweet when I got through and the shelves beneath, too. Beth helped and I tried to give her the lighter work. We did the pantry, too. That is, we made a good start.

At high noon, Beth set the table and I made some more pone. Both boys came in for dinner.

I made them wait. The man didn't come.

At last, Jim Beam leapt into the middle of the floor. "What are we waiting for?" he yelled, "I'm hungry!"

"We're waiting for your Pa." I told him.

"Pa ain't coming. Is he Beth? Is he Fly? Pa ain't coming." I looked at Beth.

"Pa don't never come in at dinnertime," she shook her head.

I jerked. No man could work all day without food. I cut the pone. "Well come to the table then," I ordered them, and I filled their tin plates. I left Beth in charge and I filled a bowl of beans and ham and tied up some hot pone. I took the water pail and dipper in the other hand.

"Where's your Pa working?"

"Dunno," Jim Beam shrugged at me between bites.

I found him. He was to the back of the house, way out, plowing. I walked over the hard ground. It sure couldn't be easy work. He whoa-ed the horse when he saw me coming.

"Din't expect you," he muttered. "Reckon'd the young'uns would tell you."

He ate every bite I brought and he took a good long drink of water. I held the bucket down for the horse to drink.

"What are you planting?"

"It oughta be corn in this ground. But we haven't got any seed," he sighed and looked out over the field.

I sloshed the rest of the water in the bottom of the pail and pushed it at the horse. He slurped it up gladly.

"I brought a little dowry," I offered.

He came to his feet. "No! I'm not taking money from a woman! You're already doing more than enough now, what with taking care of the young'uns and all."

I didn't look at him. "Hardly fitting that you don't take it, what with the young'uns coming along so fast."

He jerked.

"Flying Cloud has come home."

On the way back to the house, I scouted around some and found a shallow firepit scooped into the ground with some stones around it to set the boiler. The wash bench near it was rickety, but I reckoned I could manage on it this time. I set the boys to carrying more water and building a fire while I hunted around and dug up their dirty clothes. There were pitiful few of them, and I had to go to the barn for the man's single dirty shirt.

While I was there, I looked around and it was well made, weather-tight and for all it was so small, it would do us fine. It smelled of hay and the horse, but there wasn't hide nor hair nor sign of any kind that there was another animal on the place. No hogs, no chickens, no dog, no nothing, except that one horse.

Jim Beam and Fly tied a rope between two trees for a line for me, and Jim Beam danced and screamed and made faces in a right fine temper because I wouldn't hand him down the gun so he could go off to the woods and show Fly how good he could shoot. I tweaked a handful of his dirty, matted hair good and hard.

"Can't waste powder and shot!" I snapped. "You can show Fly the next time you go hunting. Why don't you go see did we catch anything in the snares?"

I had to put Beth to bed in my bed while I washed her dress, seeing it was the only one she had. But I wrung it out good and the breeze whipped in dry before she was ready to get up. I looked at her there in the bed and she looked like I thought a little girl should look. Clean and sweet and pretty.

I still had some time. There were three windows to the house and I sacrificed one of my Ma's best sheets to make curtains. I was quick and handy with my needle, so it didn't take long. I even whipped on a little red binding to make them look prettier.

I couldn't help but think of Gramma Hildebrand when I took out the binding. Ever since I'd known I was coming out here, she'd been bringing me things to tuck away in my trunk. This little roll of red binding, a ball of green and yellow and blue rick-rack, several spools of thread, a bit of blue ribbon, a piece of fine white lawn, a handful of narrow lace, a butter mold . . . a butter mold! That made me smile. Now, where was I going to get any butter?

"Can't tell, Lucy," she'd argue, "never know what you're gonna find. Don't reckon it'll be much. It's always best to put some things by, just in case."

Well, my trunk would hold just so much, but I crammed it as full as I could. The yarn and the needles were my own idea. And the good heavy shears . . . thinking of those shears, did I ever get Jim Beam clean, I meant to crop that mop of hair.

I plucked and drew Jim Beam's pheasants and skewered them to roast. I sorted again through the potatoes and took the best of what was left. It'd be better to plant them than eat them, so Jim Beam and Fly would be cutting eyes tomorrow. I put the poke greens to boil just as Beth stirred in the bed. Poor little mite, she sure must have been tired. Bet Jim Beam had a regular rat's nest up there in the cubby. Beth probably didn't half sleep nights.

She pulled her dress over her head quick like and, without being told, went to fetch the utensils to set the table. When she would have put on the pan of candle stubs, I shook my head and motioned at the lamp. She sat it in the middle of the table and then she admired my curtains.

"My, aren't they pretty."

I folded my dry wash down in the pantry lest the night dew wet it again, and I delved deep into the corner of my trunk and fetched forth the small leather pouch. It was money my own Ma had saved for me against the day I would marry. Five twenty-dollar gold pieces. It wasn't much, but it'd help, and we had spring and all of summer to get ready for winter. I plunked it down with a jingle before the man's plate.

That was all I had in this world except for the little I had put by myself. It was my own egg and butter money that I had earned myself, and I reckoned I'd just keep it a spell yet. It was wrapped in a bit of oilskin at the other end of my trunk.

Beth and I washed in the house, but I carried the pan out to the wash bench for the menfolk. The boys ran and swung on my rope line while they waited for their Pa to finish. He stripped off his shirt and made to really wash, and I gave him a thorough going over with my eyes for the first time, while I had the chance. He was well set up, a big man with firm, hard flesh and smooth skin. His muscles were big, his shoulders thick, his chest deep. That showed he wasn't a boy no more. His belly was flat and his hips lean. I liked that in a man. Showed health and strength.

His boots were awful worn. Mark one more thing to be done afore wintertime.

I looked at his face and it was a good face. Strong and kinda rugged-like with a wide, full mouth that could never be stingy and eyes the color of Beth's, though his had squint marks from the sun. His brows were straight and heavy and black, and his hair was a black, shaggy mane that curled a little. The skin of his face, neck, and hands was tanned darker than his body by exposure.

Not a handsome man, but a comfortable-looking one.

I handed him the clean shirt. He was surprised, but he was pleased. I summoned the boys to wash while he buttoned it and I bragged Jim Beam up a little.

"We're having roast birds for supper."

He stared at me.

"Jim Beam, he shot them."

"Yeah, Pa!" Jim Beam came up from the pan and let the water drip down his shirt front. I shoved the towel at him. "I did it, Pa! I killed 'em! Two of 'em, Pa!"

"Well, that's fine," he drawled and touched the boy's shoulder, but he looked at me kinda queer.

"Yeah! I did it!" Jim Beam was dancing, "Didn't I, Fly? Yeah! Took that ol' gun and Pow! Pow!" he aimed a pretend gun, "I killed 'em! Two of 'em! Hey, didn't I, Fly?" Jim Beam shouted. But then, Jim Beam always shouted or yelled or screamed. I wondered if perhaps he just couldn't talk normally?

Flying Cloud didn't do much better at the wash pan than Jim Beam had the first time, but I let it go. The man was still looking at me. Maybe I shouldn't have taken the gun or the powder and shot. I went back into the house.

Beth had fetched the pone to the table and was cutting it the way I showed her. She'd already lit the lamp, so I set about dishing it up.

Flying Cloud came to stand behind the stool that had been set for him next to Jim Beam. "I bring you greetings, my father," he intoned solemnly. "I bring you greetings from my grandfather, Howl-of-the-Wolf."

The man looked at him and Jim Beam interrupted. He tipped his face up to his brother's.

"Hey, Fly!" he shouted, "Can't you just say Pa?"

They both ignored him.

"Welcome, my son," the man spoke slowly, soberly.

"Howl-of-the-Wolf bids me tell you he has sent me to you now to help with the planting. After that is done, I shall return to him. He bids me say that he has done this so that I might have room in your lodge this winter when the snow flies and the wind grows cold."

The man nodded, "Howl-of-the-Wolf is wise. Eat, my son!"

Apparently, the formalities were over with. Flying Cloud sat down on his stool, came off his dignity, and ate more than Jim Beam, and that was considerable.

The man looked at the little leather poke just once, and it sat exactly where I placed it for three days. The coal oil in the lamp had been burned up for two days before he touched it.

In those three days, lots of things happened.

On that first night, I cut Beth a nightshift from the lawn, sewed it up, put it on her, and put her again to bed in the big bed. I could move her to the trundle if . . . but then, probably that wouldn't happen. I could tell by the way he looked at me when I tucked her in.

I took my knitting and my stool and went to the fire. Flying Cloud had out his knife and was showing Jim Beam how to whittle. I let them keep at it until Jim Beam cut his finger, then I tied it up and sent them both up to the cubby where I could hear them whispering.

The man sat still.

"You made curtains," he offered at last.

"I reckoned maybe, we could have outdoor shutters come wintertime."

"I reckon."

I glanced at the girl in the bed, "They are too old to all sleep together."

"I reckon," he repeated.

I waited again.

"Have we got any next neighbors?" I asked.

"Couple miles over that-a-way." He pointed.

"They good neighbors?" I was thinking along the lines of a hen and a setting of eggs.

"I reckon. I'm not thought much of around here."

I thought of Flying Cloud. No, I reckoned not. Not with a half-Indian woods-colt and so plainly marked there was no denying it.

He got up and stretched.

"I've got to mend harness again tomorrow," he paused, "Best to bar the door, there's bear and wolves around."

Wolves? Might be. Bears? Not at this time of year. I kept still though and only nodded.

He shut the door behind him.

I knit one more round. There was no sound from the cubby, the boys were asleep. I banked what was left of the fire, stood myself in the corner to undress, and crept into bed. I could feel the warmth from Beth's little body.

Well, woods-colt or not, half-Indian or not, Flying Cloud was his and so, now, he was mine. Just as Jim Beam was. Just as Beth was. Good thing too, because I guessed they were all I was going to get! No man I ever heard of would behave like that! For a man, legally wedded, to bed himself in the barn and leave his woman to her own bed alone was unheard of. Wasn't natural for a man to stay alone without a woman, and wasn't natural for a woman not to have babies of her own. I'd known some mean men, but never one this mean!

Nobody was asking for love! Not me, anyhow. Just a kind man, a good worker who tried, that's all. He didn't have to love me nor me him. I'd love his babies anyhow. Especially if they were mine too!

Well, time took care of all things. Might be, this too. Could be he was waiting to get acquainted. Humph! Looked like that would take a while!

Next day I made Beth an apron from the leftover bed sheet and I finished scrubbing the pantry. I spaded up a garden patch for planting the potato eyes come the dark of the moon. And I gave Jim Beam a bath!

I have got to say, that was no easy task! Strictly speaking, I was pretty hard put to finish the chore. But I did it!

When I told them to build a fire and put water to boil in the boiler and to put some cold in the wash tub, Jim Beam didn't suspect and he helped Fly with a right good will, stopping only to use his forefinger and thumb as a gun and yell, "Pow! Pow! Wish that rock was a deer! Pow! Shot you dead, deer! Pow! Pow! Hey, Fly! Pow!"

So, when the water in the boiler got hot, I dipped some into the tub, I got all my needs close by. I bid Beth to hide in the house and I caught Jim Beam by the arm.

He wasn't dumb and he knew right off. He fought like a wildcat and he screamed like to be heard a mile! But, like I said, I'm not a puny woman and I finally got his clothes off and jumped him into the tub. He squalled the whole time I scrubbed him.

"Ow! You're killing me! It's too hot! Ow! Now it's too cold! My skin's coming off! Ow! Ow!"

The water was getting cold. I bid Fly ladle in some more hot and then sent him to the well for a bucket of cold to rinse Jim Beam down.

"Ow! You're scalding me!"

And when Fly dumped the bucket of cold over him, he gasped for air. That didn't stop his yelling.

"Oh-h-h-h! Now you're freezing me! I'm dying! I'm kilt! Oh-h-h-h!"

He lurched around the tub so that I was nearly as sopped as he was, but I jumped him out again onto the wash bench and I scrubbed him pink and dry with the towel. I got one hand in his hair and I smacked his bottom with the other.

"You just stop that, right now, Jim Beam!" I ordered. "You put on your britches, and you set yourself down on this here bench until I get through with you, or I'll have Fly get some rope and I'll tie you down!"

He pulled on his britches, but I didn't get off that easy. If there was one thing Jim Beam could do, it was holler. "You dassen't!" he shrieked, "You wouldn't dare tie me up! You done already practically kilt me and I'm gonna be dead any minute! I'm gonna tell my Pa! Pa won't like it!"

But, under my dire threat, he sat down on the bench. I picked up my shears.

"Hold still!"

"Naw!" he shouted, "Ain't gonna! You're gonna cut off my neck! I'm gonna tell my Pa! Pa won't like it!"

I pulled his hair enough to make him look at me. "I aim to cut your hair, Jim Beam," I told him calmly. "Of course, that depends on you. Just keep squirming around and might be I will cut off your neck!"

I snapped the blades of the shears a couple of times and I have never seen a boy sit so still. Of course, he was like to bust afore I was through. I popped the towel and brushed the hair from his neck and back.

It had been a real ordeal for him. I saw tears beginning to form in his eyes. Well, sure after all that I wasn't gonna let Jim Beam disgrace himself.

"That's fine, Jim Beam," I bragged him up, "That's just fine. Now, if you're not too *kilt*, let's just go in and get the gun. I reckon maybe you could bring in a couple more birds today."

That was all. He skinned into his shirt in nothing flat! His strut was just as cocky as ever.

He had entirely forgotten he was *"kilt"*.

"Hey, Fly, come on!" he shouted, "Gonna get that ol' gun! Gonna get a deer! Er, might be a grizzly bear! Hey, Fly! Hey, Mr. Bear! Pow! Pow! Come on, Fly!"

Jim Beam was restored in all. I hadn't hurt his dignity a bit. Sure improved his looks though. He was nearly as light-skinned as Beth now he was clean.

Fly was a different matter. I reckon he took pride in holding a straight face, but this time he couldn't quite cut it. There was a funny look in his eyes and he acted a little dazed like. Bet he'd never seen anything like that before!

I caught myself looking at his dirty buckskins and his lank greasy hair. I jerked myself up.

I couldn't dare to scrub him and I'd as well cut off his neck as his hair!

Beth was all eyes as she dashed up to us. "I heard you, Jim Beam!" she laughed, "I heard you yelling!"

I caught her. "Wasn't anything," I told her, "Jim Beam was just taking a bath."

He didn't even hear me. Because of his bath, I let him prepare six loads for the gun.

"Are you taking that many?" I warned him sternly, "You bring back what you don't use. You hear me, Jim Beam, we'll have no waste!"

But it was no use to talk to him. I put Fly in mind to check the snares, and off they went. Several hours later, they came back heralded by Jim Beam's shouting. He carried three pheasants this time and the gun. Fly carried two rabbits my four snares had netted and, of all things, a nest of eggs!

I cuddled them in a piece of wool flannel I was saving against a good chest cold in one of the young'uns. I turned them with the flat of my palms before I covered them. Not too likely, but maybe, I could hatch out some of them. Just one rooster and two, three hens and we'd have our own pheasants.

I sent Jim Beam and Fly to the field with their Pa's dinner and the water pail. Jim Beam hollered a protest the first time I told him.

"Well," I drawled at him, "I've never heard of any boy eating before his Pa. If the Pa don't eat, the boy don't eat!" I didn't have to say it twice.

We had rabbit for supper that night and Flying Cloud pegged out their pelts on the barn wall.

Next night we had pheasant again and the candles sputtered out, their wicks burned up in their own grease.

The man took the little leather poke of money.

Chapter Four

Next day I got up early. I fixed a real out-sized breakfast. The man didn't look at me all through it.

When he stomped out of the house, I hurried myself. I jumped Beth up as best I could, with her clean dress and white apron. Then I brushed her hair until it shown. I tied off her braids with the blue ribbon. I scatted the boys outside and dressed myself clean. I left my apron off. I took my marriage shawl, but I could not squeeze my feet into those new shoes. I redid my hair and I took some money out of the oiled-skin packet and slid it into my pocket.

I left Jim Beam in charge of the house and Fly in charge of the nest of eggs and Jim Beam.

Taking Beth firmly by the hand, I went for a visit to our next neighbors.

I could see the place long before we got there. It was fenced around with a white fence. At least, the front of the house was. Chickens scratched in the yard, pigs rooted in a pen, cows mooed from the barn, and when I got to the gate I had to stop and stare.

A dog barked and bayed and lunged viciously the length of its chain. It was a hound dog alright, but there was something else mixed in. It was bigger than any hound dog I'd ever seen and more vicious, too.

Yet when the little fat woman spoke to it from the door, it slunk down quiet, though it still bared its teeth at me.

"Howdy!" the woman called.

"Howdy," I spoke up. "Admire your dog. Had puppies recently, hasn't she?"

She stepped out a little, "I see ya' knows dawgs." She wiped her hands on her apron. "Be ya' neighbors?"

"Next neighbors," I answered.

"Oh," she looked at Beth, "ya' be Roan Shields' new wife?"

"I'm Miz Shields," I admitted. "You're the closest neighbor, and I came asking for a little help."

"Help?" She came a couple more steps into the yard.

"Well, Shields' don't beg," I stated firmly.

She turned back towards the house. "Adam!" she called, "Adam! Oh! Oh! Adam!"

I gave Beth's hand a sharp squeeze so she wouldn't gawk.

The man rounded the corner of the house. He was thin and stringy and sorta loose moving.

He sided up next to his wife.

"This here's Roan Shields' new wife. She's a-callin' on us as next neighbors, Adam," the woman explained.

I don't know why she called him. I could have done my business with her because I did anyhow, in the end. I got a deep breath and I walked right by the nose of that hound.

"Howdy," I said, "I'm Miz Shields. And this here's Beth."

The man cleared his throat, "Howdy." His Adam's apple wobbled, "I'm Adam Colbey. This here's m' wife, Alice."

I nodded, "Mr. Colbey, I came over to see if you can help us out. We've got young'uns over to the Square Heap and we need some livestock. If you have any to spare, I reckon I'd like to take a look."

He swallowed hard, "Ya' meanin' ter buy, Miz Shields?"

"If you have anything that I want to buy," I told him.

He perked up and stuck his thumbs in his britches band, "Ya' wants a cow?"

"Umm." I grunted. "I sort of reckoned on a goat. A young one with her first kid. You can keep the kid. I get breeding rights back to your billy and you get the kid. Twins, I keep one."

He goggled. Well, now he knew I knew what I was about. I let him have it.

"A hen. One setting on eggs. You guarantee me a rooster." I stared down my nose at him, "I'll give you hard cash."

His manner changed altogether. He couldn't do enough for me.

"Alice, ya' hear? Come on in, Miz Shields, come on in," he laid hold of my arm.

"I reckon not," I shook off his hand. "If you have what I want, I'll buy. Let's take a looksee."

He sorta danced behind me and his wife led the way. She pointed out all the virtues of the livestock. I knew it was not so. Some of their stock was good, most of it was bad. I picked the best.

I picked out a goat. It wasn't her first kid, but she was the youngest they had and her udder was good. She was newly freshened. I picked a big red hen and her nest of fourteen eggs.

Miz Colbey tried to sell me every animal on the place. I turned down the litter of piglets.

On second thought, I took one. It was big enough to eat if we couldn't raise it.

I didn't haggle the price because the man blurted it out before his wife could. It was more than fair. I clinched it before she could retract his generosity.

Then we passed the litter of puppies. Beth went down on her knees and pushed her tiny hand among the wriggling pups. I stopped.

"I'd admire to have one of those pups," I stated.

The woman cut her man off, "Which one?"

"The runt bitch," I answered instantly.

"She'll cost ya' five dollars," the woman was shrewd.

And so, Beth and I started back for home. The piglet was under one of my arms, the hen under the other. The nest of eggs tied in a bundle at my wrist. The goat pulled on a lead rope from my elbow and Beth carried the puppy.

Seemed shorter coming home than going. Reckon I tried Beth's strength, but I was anxious about Jim Beam. I wanted to get this setting of eggs settled. The hen squawked dismally. The goat brayed, the piglet squealed and wriggled. The puppy slept.

Worn out or not, Beth skipped the last few steps across the yard. "Jim Beam! Jim Beam! Fly! Look at what we got!"

I frowned when there was no answer from the Square. She shrieked fit to wake the dead!

I threw open the door to the house and it was empty of boys! They were nowhere to be found.

I stood there with the hen and the piglet and the bawling goat and I've got to say my temper came up. It had been a long, hot, and not pleasant trip, and I had expected some help when I got home. I had thought to put the goat, the piglet, and the hen in the barn and I had counted on the boys' help.

There wouldn't be no dinner to get to speak of. The man would be gone the day. Perhaps more. The young'uns could have pone, goat's milk, and leavings from last night's supper.

Now it was anybody's guess. Could be the boys wouldn't show up to eat. Could be they would show up when they got good and ready. Well, Jim Beam could depend on it, he'd sure get his come-uppance.

I lifted my eyes. The gun was gone from its place. Oh, yes! Jim Beam would sure catch hob.

"You go inside with the puppy," I told Beth. "I've got to put these others in the barn. I'll be back directly. You wait for me."

She seemed glad to comply. How had this wee wisp managed before I'd come?

Disgusted, I dumped the piglet in the grain bin. There wasn't nothing in it anyhow, but he seemed contented to root around. I had to tether the goat and I set the hen to nesting in a heaped up pile of straw in a corner. She scratched and turned her eggs and clucked to herself, but she finally settled down with an indignant ruffle of her feathers. I shook my head. I should have been more shrewd. She could have covered twice as many.

I prodded the goat's udder with my finger and decided against milk for dinner. Leave her be and we get a full measure for supper. If the boys came in, they'd get some pone. Just plain pone.

Fly alone would have done just as I bid him. But with Jim Beam to urge and to lead, who knew what was happening. And the gun was gone, too!

I took that hard. I was the one who'd let Jim Beam shoot. I had given him the gun. It was up to me to make sure he used it well. He'd not take it again so easy. I'd make sure of that.

I went back to the house and turned the pheasant eggs. And then I carried water for everything on the place, filling the barrel in the horse's stall because I knew he'd need it when he came in. I even carried water to that silly pup who had to have Beth's wet fingers shoved into her mouth to teach her to drink. She wasn't weaned! I crumbled a bit of pone in water for her, but Beth had to practically push it down her throat. She went to sleep right off, her ugly little nose shoved up against my nest of pheasant eggs.

Beth and I ate.

"What should we call her, Ma?" she demanded.

"Why, I reckon she belongs to us all," I told her. "Why don't you name her, Beth? You toted her home."

She pinked up with pleasure. But she took her time. She puzzled a long while. We were redding up the kitchen when she spoke again.

"Do you reckon she was lost, Ma?"

"Lost?"

"Well, with all the other ones. Don't you reckon they would have pushed her out?"

"I reckon they would," I saw what she was driving at, "most likely she'd have starved."

"Hm-mmm." She nodded solemnly, "Then I think we should call her "Lost Be.""

I supposed she was right. "Lost Be," I repeated. "Why, that's right pretty, Beth."

Her face lit up and she went to grasp the fat, wiggly, sleepy pup in her arms. And so she helped me with the rest of the chores, stopping after each one to cuddle and stroke Lost Be, who couldn't have cared less.

The moon would be dark that night. I planted my potatoes, hoeing the rows with Beth following to drop in the eyes. I backtracked, covering them just right, and then carried water by the bucketful to water them. Maybe they really didn't need the water, but I had to make sure.

We'd sure need those potatoes come winter.

I went back to the house with Beth for a cool drink of water. I eyed Lost Be uneasily.

Every time she put her head down, she nuzzled that warm nest.

I took three of the pheasant eggs, keeping them warm in my hands, and went off to the barn.

The hen ruffled her feathers, clucked, and offered to peck me.

"Now, Biddy," I soothed, "oh, come on now Biddy." I slipped the three eggs under her. If she took to them, I'd add the rest as fast as I could. Looked like maybe she would, for she didn't raise up on her legs, just ruffled her feathers and "pucked" at me. I left her alone.

Beth had followed me and she watched in silent awe while I knelt by the goat and milked into a clean lard pail. I gave the Nanny some hay on the ground. The first thing I needed was a manger for the goat. Mark one!

The piglet squealed and scrabbled in the grain bin. I added a little of the warm milk to the bowl of leavin's, everything that I'd been able to gather, and put a handful into the lard pail lid for the hen. Next a trough for Biddy, and a nest. Mark two!

I fished the shoat out of the grain bin and put it to its pan. The food literally vanished. I put it back and it scrabbled and squealed just the same. A grain bin was no place for a pig. Sty, wallow, trough. Mark three!

I carried the milk pail back to the house. Beth followed hobbledy-hoy alongside and, at last, she thrust a finger into the white foam. She stuck it in her mouth and stared up at me.

"What's that?" she whispered.

Poor mite! I suspect her Pa had done as best he could, but her Ma? Must be nearly seven or eight, and she didn't know milk! Poor mite!

"That's milk," I told her. "You make cheese out of it. You put it on your mush, and you drink it. It's good and it's good for you, too. You can make a lot of things out of it. We'll just go in and strain it out and hang it down the well and you'll see. It will be cool and fresh and really good."

Supper was well on and twilight near when Jim Beam and Fly came home. I could hear Jim Beam shouting nearly from the edge of the woods.

When Beth would have run out, I motioned to her sternly. She fell back and crouched on the hearth clinging to the pup.

The door slammed back under Jim Beam's heavy hand. "Hey!" he shouted, "Hey, Beth! Ma! Look at us! Hey!"

I turned from the side board prepared to quell him with a stern eye, with silent action. I didn't do it. I stared and surely my jaw dropped.

Both of them were dirtier than I had ever thought boys could be! Rivulets of blood turned black on Fly's buckskins and sopped Jim Beam's shirt in great brackish red splotches. Blood smeared his face and hands, but he marched triumphantly to the table and clapped down the powder horn and shot.

"There!" He shouted, "There, Ma!" He took a stance, feet wide straddled, gun butt against his foot, the muzzle swung wide in his stained fist.

He shouted again. "Hey! Me and Fly got us a deer! Killed it. Dead! Brung you the meat! A whole deer!"

I tried to draw myself up. They couldn't be hurt, neither of them, from the way they were acting. "I don't see a deer," I said sternly.

"Aw!" cried Jim Beam, "We didn't bring it here! Everybody knows you've got to hang a deer. We got it hung up in the woods."

"Hung!" Was it possible these two boys could have hung a deer? I could have been inclined to disbelieve Jim Beam, but one look at Fly's shining face convinced me. Yes, by golly, they had got themselves a deer.

Of course, that did not excuse Jim Beam! Deer or no deer, he had taken the gun without permission. I taught him his lesson immediately.

I deliberately stepped across to him and I caught the gun from his hand. I put it back on its prongs over the hearth.

"Get inside and wash!" I ordered sternly from the doorway. "You can't come to the table like that."

He stared at me as though he could not believe his ears. "Aw!" he screamed in sudden fury, "I'm not gonna tell you where it is! Won't! Leave him hang! I wish I didn't shoot that old deer! I won't tell you where it is!"

"Go wash!" I repeated sharply and turned my back to dish up.

They washed. Jim Beam deliberately went light on the water. He came to the table with a sullen, stained face and his sticky-stiff shirt.

Fly had made an effort. His jerkin showed obvious swipes with a wet cloth. He held a silent, closed face and took his place with no word.

Jim Beam scowled and glowered and refused to eat. From the way Fly shoveled in the food, I knew Jim Beam must be starved. Nevertheless, he did not take one morsel of food from his plate.

It stung me because I knew he needed the food, and especially the milk. Fly drank his with plain relish. He knew milk. Beth tasted hers delicately, flashed her eyes and grinned, and really dove in. Milk might be new to her, but she took to it with a will.

When we had finished, Beth knelt on the hearth, and with tears in her eyes, offered Lost Be in her arms to her brother. He aimed a wicked kick at the pup and fled up the ladder and across the plank to the cubby.

Beth cuddled the yipping little hound, her tears falling on the soft fur and Fly made the first sympathetic move I had ever seen him make. He did not touch the puppy, but he laid a hand on his sister's shoulder. He caught a tear from her cheek upon his forefinger and rubbed it away with the tips of his other fingers. He did not look at me but followed Jim Beam up to the cubby.

I washed and wiped that night and left Beth to cuddle her pup. Lost Be quieted right down and it was not she who suffered. I fixed her leavings and added a bit of milk, and I set Beth to feeding her.

I could not back down. I was beginning to understand Jim Beam. I set my teeth and I made it stick.

Chapter Five

The man came back next morning. I had first been to the barn. I had fed the animals and I had milked the goat. I could see him coming in, so I hurried.

I shook Beth up and got her dress on her and I brushed and braided her hair quickly.

I flipped a small stick of kindling wood up into the cubby. "Jim Beam! Fly!" I put a stern note into my voice, "Your Pa's home! Get down here and help him if you want any breakfast!"

They were down faster than I thought they could be. A godsend that Jim Beam healed so easily. And with his nature, he had need to. When the man pulled up before the door, we were all waiting.

The horse looked tired, the man looked tired and I would have bet he was hungry. He climbed over the seat into the wagon bed and began unloading parcels. I motioned the boys. Jim Beam couldn't wait.

"Pa!" he yelled, "Hey, Pa! You just should have been here, Pa! You ain't going to like it! You just wait! I'm going to tell you all about it, Pa!"

Well, I reckon Jim Beam was going to tell him, but he wasn't going to tell just now.

"You just get the wagon unloaded, Jim Beam! You can tell later, after your Pa's eaten."

Jim Beam flashed his eyes at me, but he didn't stop hollering. He simply changed the subject.

"Hey, Pa! This here's heavy! What did you bring, Pa? Whew! You must have bought out the store! Hey, Pa, are we rich?"

The man led the horse away to the barn and there were still some sacks left in the rickety wooden bed.

I let him go. The mush was boiling, the water was boiling for chicory, and there was milk to be pulled up from the well.

He came back from the barn just in time for the hot, dished-up meal. He got a cup of milk along with his chicory. He looked at me strangely, but he didn't say anything.

He really didn't have a chance. Jim Beam gave a shouted account of all that had happened to him since his Pa had left.

Again, I didn't listen. Wee little Lost Be waddled beneath the table and nosed us all. Jim Beam interrupted himself to shout, "Hey, Dog!" And he carried her between outstretched hands to the door.

Beth squiggled in her chair. I could tell by the tuck of her little lips that she was happy.

She could enjoy Lost Be only if Jim Beam did.

There was a very strong link between Beth and Jim Beam. They both welcomed Flying Cloud, but apparently, he was accustomed to coming and going freely, according to the whims of Howl-of-the-Wolf. All of the young'uns seemed attached to each other, but the unconscious bond between Beth and her natural, legal, fullblood brother was very strong. Jim Beam was fully aware of this, but he was belligerent, egotistical, pro-man aware. It must have been hard for Jim Beam to live up to this trust. But he tried! Oh, indeed, how he did try.

I cleared my throat. "You'll not be plowing today?" I asked the man.

Lock-jawed, he shook his head. "Horse is wore out," he muttered.

And he was, too. I wondered if he's slept at all since he'd left us.

I frowned at Jim Beam to shut his mouth. "Be quiet, Jim Beam!" I ordered sharply, "Your Pa'll rest a while on the bed, and you and Fly and Beth and me, we'll go out to the barn and fix up for the animals."

"Animals?" He screamed and leapt away from the table to dance in the middle of the floor, "What animals?"

"Well, now, you and Fly just go out and have a look. And Beth and I will come soon, and I'll show you what's to be done."

"Don't need you to show me nothing," Jim Beam shouted. "Can do! Me and Fly can do!"

Fly pulled away from the table. He was siding Jim Beam. I wondered why. Fly was at least a year older than Jim Beam. Why did he follow Jim Beam rather than assert himself as the eldest?

He followed Jim Beam. I let them go. I wanted to speak to the man.

He drained his cup of milk. "You got a goat?" he lifted tired eyes.

"And a piglet and a hen and fourteen eggs and Lost Be," I indicated, the puppy who again was nuzzling at the pheasant nest on the hearth.

"Next neighbors?" his eye glinted.

Oh, I knew that look. "Shields's don't beg," I told him. "I *bought* them from our next neighbors, the Colbeys, with my own money. Good buys, too. All excepting that fool pup."

His eyes turned to Beth and he seemed to slump all of a sudden.

"You just have off your boots and rest a while in the bed," I told him. "There's plenty for us to do outside."

"No," he protested, "I'll help."

He rose up and I laid a hand to his shoulder. I shook my head, "You have got to have some rest. We can manage." I met his eyes, "You, above all, have got to keep your strength up."

He didn't say anything more and I motioned Beth to fetch Lost Be. Well, you could always bet on Jim Beam to keep things lively. It must have been Fly who climbed into the bin and handed out the piglet, because it was a shrieking Jim Beam who burst running from the barn two jumps behind the squealing, terrified shoat.

"Catch him! Catch him!" Now I was shrieking just as loudly as Jim Beam. There went the promise of hams, side-pork, hogs-head cheese, and pickled pig's feet on the hoof! Not to mention half-a-dozen other things. Jim Beam's deer wouldn't make up for the loss of that squealing little runt!

"Stop, Hog!" screeched Jim Beam. "I'm gonna get you'! Stay still, you dumb Hog! I'm gonna get you!"

Fly appeared at Jim Beam's heels, and yelling and running the four of us chased that pig. He ran right by Beth twice before she had sense enough to put down Lost Be. Seemed like we chased that pig a long time before Jim Beam made a flying leap, knocked me flat in the dirt, and caught him.

Folding up my legs and smoothing out my apron, I sat there to catch my breath. "Get up off that pig!," I told Jim Beam.

He got up, the wiggling, squealing piglet clutched tight, upside down, against his chest. "See that, Hog!" he shouted, panting. "I told you so! I said I was gonna get you! And I got you, didn't I, Hog? Hey, Hog! I got you!"

I got up, dusted off my dress, and looked toward the house. The man was standing in the door watching. Well, reckon there wasn't much dignity in a grown woman shrieking and chasing a pig, but first things first. First full stomachs, and then dignity. We'd saved the pig and that was what counted.

Of course, I'd lost three pheasant eggs in the process. They were cracked and spilled on the ground and looked real mussy.

"Put the shoat back in the grain bin until we get a sty built." I ordered Jim Beam, and I got the spade and cleaned up the eggs.

I hoed three rows so that, using the barn wall for the back, I had a neat square.

"Aw!" shouted Jim Beam, "What's that for? You ain't going to dig a pit, are you?"

"Don't reckon." I sorted through the scant pile of sawed lumber behind the barn. It was weathered good. Left over from when the barn was built, I supposed, for that was the only planking on the place.

I found some four-by-fours and Jim beam sawed them all off even. I've got to say his cuts weren't exactly straight, but he sawed with a right good will. It turned out, once we'd set the posts, that he was better with the hammer, so I did the sawing. My cuts weren't much straighter, but the sty would be serviceable and didn't need to be pretty. I didn't reckon on it being permanent anyhow.

We made the fence three planks high, the widest set in my hoed rows, and spaces between them. It looked fine to me, but Jim Beam felt different.

"That ain't no good!" he shouted, "It won't work! That old Hog'll get right out!"

I wiped my damp forehead. "Now, you just listen to me, Jim Beam! Ol' Hog ain't going no place at all. By the time he gets big enough to crawl over that first board, he's gonna be too big to get through the slot."

He studied on that and then he hollered again, "You didn't make no gate! You didn't."

I brushed off my hands, swiped back my hair, and tried to be patient with him. "Do I want to get in, I'll just step over. If you want to get in, you can climb."

Beth laughed right out and Fly turned his back kinda sudden-like. Jim Beam opened his mouth. I got there first, "Jim Beam, you and Fly go get Hog and put him in here. I reckon it'll stop his scrabbling even if it doesn't stop his squealing."

They dashed away, and this time Fly carried Hog. Jim Beam scrambled over the fence and took the piglet and set him down. "There, Hog!" he yelled, "There! Your new home Hog! Hey! You like it? Hey, Hog!"

I set Fly to whittling with his knife, mitering the edges of a couple of short planks for a trough. Jim Beam and I argued our way through the building of a square box nest for Biddy. She squawked some when I moved her eggs, but she scratched them around to suit her and settled down right comfortable.

Then there was only the goat left. She bleated at me dismally. Well, she'd have to be staked out for now, the sun was high overhead and dinner was to get. It had taken more time than I reckoned, but it was a good morning's work, considering the help I'd had.

All four of us staked out the goat.

"Yaah! She's got a gray beard!" Jim Beam shrieked, and danced in front of her, "Yaah! You ol' gray bearded goat!"

I could have told him better, but there are some young'uns who just have to learn. She lowered her little head and butted him a good one right in the stomach. He rolled around on the ground and yelled fit to die. I knew he wasn't hurt, just the breath knocked out of him. I let him roll.

Fly laid a hand to one of her curved horns and gently pulled her head around. "She has moon eyes," he said softly. "She is a good little beast."

When Jim Beam got through rolling around on the ground and yelling, I faced him flatly, "You spent six shots worth of powder and ball on that deer. We're all trying to do our part. Your Pa's tired, and a man needs meat. Now, what do you say, Jim Beam?"

"Aw!" he screamed, "Forgot that ol' deer! Sure, let's eat the ol' deer! I killed him, Ma! Me and Fly! I reckon Pa would like a piece of ol' deer! Yeah!"

"Well," I drawled, "I reckon a man who does the best he can fer his young'uns would like to get his teeth into a nice piece of meat once in a while. Now, suppose he has a boy who's got meat, but doesn't want to share it . . . ."

Beth gasped. "Oh, Jim Beam!" she cried, "You wouldn't! You wouldn't!"

Jim Beam danced about, his face red and contorted. "Yeah!" he screamed, "Yeah! I do! Killed ol' deer to eat! Hung up ol' deer to eat! I told you I got that ol' deer for meat! I told you . . . ."

He was getting too excited. I interrupted him very quietly, "I reckon, we'd best go get that old deer then, Jim Beam. Horse is tired, but he'll do this."

We took the horse and went to fetch the deer. I took along a shovel just in case, but I should have known Fly would know better than to leave entrails around. A small animal had been at the carcass. Fly sliced it away with his knife.

Between us we got the deer on the horse's back. The horse shied and balked, but we managed back to the house. We let it down on the wash bench. It was a small buck. I borrowed Fly's knife and sliced deeply into the loin.

He caught my arm with strong tense fingers. "Forgive me, my mother, but you spoil the skin."

He had never spoken directly to me. It startled me so that I relinquished the knife. "Skin it out as you please," I answered him, "but get me half a dozen chops quick."

I went into the house and stirred up the fire. I looked at the bed. The man slept with abandon, all sprawled out. He heard me and moved right now.

I pushed the spider in and set the skillet to heat. "Jim Beam got a deer yesterday." I told him.

"Jim Beam? A deer?" His voice was thick with sleep.

"Rouse up, Mr. Shields," I dared say it, "I reckon we won't work too much more today. Horse is tired. You are tired. We can plow and plant tomorrow."

He grunted. It was alright. I hadn't overstepped. I had an awful habit of overstepping. Fly and Jim Beam burst through the door with the dripping meat in their hands.

"On the sideboard! On the sideboard!" I called.

Beth followed with Lost Be in her arms. She crossed the floor shyly and turned that pup loose on the crazy quilt on my bed! I crossed my fingers.

The man caught up his girl-child and the pup. "Dogs have got to be on ground," he chided her, "especially pups."

And I saw him grin for the first time. It was surprisingly pleasant.

I made pone and we dined royally on red meat. It must have been the first they had had in a long while. I cut Beth's and she tasted it gingerly. Then she closed her eyes and squiggled her nose in ecstasy. "Thank you, Jim Beam! Thank you! It's wonderful!"

I stared at her. Any one of my brothers would have thought I had lost my wits did I thank them so for meat on the table. One look at Jim Beam's face convinced me that Beth sensed strange hidden things. He needed this praise as desperately as he needed a smack on the bottom at times.

She didn't give her praise to Fly. He didn't need it.

"It's right good to have meat," I told him. And just so he wouldn't get too smartified, I added, "I hope you'll be able to do this good all summer and Fly shows you how to gut and skin them properly."

There, that showed Fly I knew his part. It was wasted though; he flashed his eyes knowingly. This wasn't Fly's first deer. It struck me that he knew exactly what was going on here, and that he understood completely. He knew a family relationship that had never existed here in the Square Heap!

I dared again, "How do you like the meat, Mr. Shields?"

"What," His eyes shot to me and I dropped my own and kept on chewing. He said nothing more.

Humph! He must be still sluggish from sleep!

Beth lifted her cup, "It's so good, Ma." She drank deep, "I reckon we have to thank little Moon Eyes too."

See, there she went again. I'd been raised on a farm all my life. I'd had a lot to do with young'uns, my brothers' young'uns, and I'd dealt with animals since I was able to walk. How come this child was showing me the way?

I clanked the pans harder than need be when I washed up. The man lingered at the table. I snapped out at Jim Beam. "Moon Eyes needs to have a manger. We can tether her if we have to, but she's got to have a manger."

The man rose and stretched. My, he was big! I didn't look. "Fly, you and Jim Beam come on. We'll fix up something for the . . . for Moon Eyes." They followed him out.

That's how the goat came to be Moon Eyes. Beth's gift to Flying Cloud and it was their secret. Jim Beam never did know.

Chapter Six

They built the manger; and the man quartered the deer, wiped it down with cool water from the well, and hung it in the pantry within easy reach so I could cut what I wanted from it.

Beth and I unpacked the bundles he had brought. He'd used good judgment. There were the basic necessities, more corn meal, lard, beans, grits, a small sack of white flour, a tiny tin box of tea, coffee, chicory, salt, and a bucket of black strap. There was a big can of coal oil, a poke of oats for porridge, a packet of good big candles, some dried prunes, some raisins, and some baking powder. There were some packets of seeds: turnips, onions, snap beans, cabbage, and tomatoes.

He must have had help with the rest for there were several lengths of cloth, some spools of thread, and a handful of buttons.

I could not see where he had spent one cent foolishly.

I made a raisin pie. There was no corn starch, so I boiled them off with a little extra sugar to cover the taste of the flour I'd have to use to thicken them. I was used to a baking chamber, but I didn't have one now. I made do with the big iron pot, hanging it on the crane, setting the pie inside, and putting the heavy lid on tight. It worked out fine.

Beth had a way of squinching in upon herself, wrinkling her nose, slitting her eyes, drawing up her cheeks, and squirming ecstatically when she was pleased. She performed these actions several times while she ate her wedge of pie.

Jim Beam held back from gobbling, just barely, but he ate so fast as he figured he could get away with. When his pan was clean, he stared at me.

"What was that?" he demanded.

How like Jim Beam to eat it first and enjoy it after. "That's pie. I'll make more one day."

"Pie!" he yelled, "I ain't never heard of no pie afore! But it's good! Gooder than most anything. I like pie, I do!"

The man drained his cup and pushed his pan away. "Mighty fine!" he pronounced. "Haven't had pie in a coon's age."

Fly stared me square in the eye, "My mother cooks nearly as well as the squaw of Howl-of-the-Wolf."

I blinked. Guess he felt called upon to add his bit. No doubt, he'd enjoyed the sweet, but he was used to Indian cooking and that sure was something I knew nothing about at all!

No use for me to say I wasn't pleased, because I sure was. I'd been cooking a good many years. I'd never had, and never expected to have, anything good said about any chore I did, but I could sure count on being taken up short if things weren't just right.

Growing up with four brothers on a farm in Indiana, I'd pulled my weight just like the rest of them, doing any farm chore that came to hand and housework besides. After Papa died, I took care of Momma as the boys got married and moved out, all except Buck, of course. As the eldest, he brought his bride, Becky, home to take over the farm, and his family became my responsibility, too. When Momma died,

I was passed around among my brothers, from farm to farm, for the work I could do.

Oh, suppose my brothers cared for me, at least, some of them did, but they had their own places, their own work, their own wives and young'uns, and so there was never much affection left over for me. I always had a roof over my head and enough to eat, but I had to work for it. I'd have got the same if they'd put me out for a bound-girl.

That was really how I'd happened to come to this wilderness they call Missouri. That was how it had happened that I had married Roan Shields and come to the Square Heap.

It was in 1875, on my twenty-fifth birthday, that I pulled up my head and looked around me. They all had homes and families. I was the only one who had nothing.

My hand had never been asked in marriage. My brothers saw to that. They had driven off any man that looked at me twice. Lucy didn't need to marry. She had everything she needed. And they needed Lucy to pass around between them to do whatever chore was necessary. I was a good, hard worker and they never failed to call on me for any job that needed doing. If a baby was to be birthed, get Lucy! If a wife was ailing, get Lucy! And Lucy was as good as a man in the fields any day.

On that day, when I was twenty-five, I made up my mind not to wait anymore. Lucy did need a man, a home, and young'uns of her own, and Lucy was going to get them. I didn't know exactly what I was going to do or how. I just knew I was going to do it.

I had a little education. I was sociable. I wasn't beautiful, but I cleaned up right good.

Plus being strong and willing . . . well, there just had to be a way out.

At that time, I was staying with Buck, my oldest brother. I'd been there three months, first because Becky was birthing her eighth young'un and then, though he was now past two months old, she still wasn't up and doing. She was dragging and whining and playing off just like she always did when I was around. You have no notion how she could take hold and what a strong hand she wielded when Lucy wasn't there to do it for her.

It was odd that it was Buck that brought the paper home. He came in that very night from an afternoon in town and he'd been lapping it up in the saloon. I could tell because he was all sweaty, his yellow hair standing every which-a-way, and his face all pink. He slapped the paper down on the table next to Becky's elbow.

"See what some damn fool's posting all over town ," he bellowed with a laugh. "Ain't that a damn fool thing?"

She began to whine at him and pick and he began to deny that he'd drunk anything stronger than water. When she commanded me to *"throw that fool paper in the fire,"* I sneaked it into my pocket instead. Why? Because it said on the top of it in great big black letters "WIVES WANTED."

I got supper over with. I didn't listen to the quarreling of Buck and Becky. The young'uns squalled and brawled among themselves and I should have smacked some of them soundly. I did not. I just hurried as fast as I could so I could get alone and read that paper.

It was printed big and little, dark and light, thick and thin, so it took me a while to study it out. It all boiled down to one fact. A Mister Burtram Thompson was soliciting to find wives for what he termed *"the brave pioneers of our great country."* It would seem that these daring, courageous men had ventured forth, had hewed out homes and were building towns. They needed the help of good women. Passage was to be paid and marriage guaranteed upon arrival for any good woman willing to aid these pioneers. The men were listed below, but the paper didn't give very much information.

They were listed like this:

1: PETE BURNET - aged 30 - bachelor - leaves with wagon train out of St. Jo. September 1876 for California

2: LANE PERVIS - aged 45 - bachelor - leaves with wagon train out of St. Jo. September 1876 for California

3: PEALEY SMITH - aged 60 - bachelor - preacher/small parish Oregon Territory

4: ROAN SHIELDS - aged 30 - widower - **and family** - good farm in Missouri

5: JACK BUCKETTE - aged 29 - bachelor - Deputy Sheriff - Oklahoma Territory

6: WHITEY MANN - aged 40 - widower - traveling medicine show - no family

I read the list over and over. I don't know why I did. There was only one choice for me. I didn't know anything but farming and I knew enough of that not to want to start from scratch. That let out Lane Pervis and Pete Burnet.

I didn't want to live in any town and being a deputy wasn't a safe job. I might be a widow before I was a wife. That let out Jack Buckette.

Pealey Smith's age let him. Whitey Mann, I didn't even consider. I didn't hanker to live out of a wagon.

That left Roan Shields . . . *and family.*

I examined myself carefully in the glass. My hair was paler even than Buck's and hung to my hips, and when I plaited it into one braid at night it was nearly as thick as Buck's wrist. My skin had lost some of its summer tan and my eyes were more hazel than brown. Funny I should have such dark brows and lashes, with such pale hair.

Maybe it wasn't a pretty face, but it was passable. And I was big and strong and had a good ten years of child bearing before me yet.

I screwed up my courage and I wrote to Mr. Burtram Thompson, unbeknownst to my brothers. He answered me, I wrote to him again and he answered again before the arrangements were made. It was only then when the date for me to leave was set that I told them.

Half of them were mad and the other half scoffed. I didn't let them bother me and I paid no attention to the squawking's of their wives. All except Becky. When she screeched at me, I told her tartly to tell Buck to get her a bound-girl. That shut the mouths of the others. Becky wouldn't even say goodbye to me.

Gramma Hildebrand, our old neighbor lady, was the only one who had tried to help me. And the best she could do was to give me her old carpet bag and $2.00 that she had saved up out of her egg money.

And now, here I was, married to Roan Shields. I had a man of my own, and a family, and a farm. The Square Heap! They needed me. They wanted me. And this was mine. No use for me to say it didn't please me when they appreciated what I did. You bet it did!

Chapter Seven

The next day we planted.

The man drove the horse and laid his weight to the plow to make the furrows. Fly didn't need any telling and curbed his brother with single words. That left just Beth and me. We worked next rows and I carried the seed for us both caught up in my apron.

I smiled when I saw it was corn. I poured from my apron into Beth's and went back to take the hoe and cover the rows. Amazingly enough, it was Fly who followed me, working odd rows as we kept up. Jim Beam and Beth dropping seed as the man plowed and us covering.

We planted that field in one day. Maybe it wasn't big, but it was big enough. It would provide food for us and for the horse, goat, and pig. Some for Biddy, too. We were all tired, but it was a good tiredness. We went early to bed.

We had porridge the next morning with sugar and milk, and it was good. I made a big pot and they ate it all. The young'uns drank milk, but the man and I drank pure coffee. It was sure a treat after so much straight chicory. Of course, I wasn't going to be that extravagant all the time. I'd stretch the coffee with chicory for everyday drinking, but I was going to save some out to have pure on occasion.

The tea I knew for what it was. A present to me. It was precious and would be used only very rarely, or might be, in case of sickness.

Over our second cups, I looked at the man, "Do you think you can get by with just the boys today, Mr. Shields?" I asked.

He looked at me like he thought I was sick. "Are you ailing, Miz Shields?" he frowned.

"Of course not! I just reckoned I'd best get in the rest of the truck garden. Turnips and onions leastwise, while the moon's still dark. Got washing to do, too, but I expect I could help after dinner . . . Mr. Shields."

Jim Beam scraped his bowl and thunked his spoon on the table. Color came up on the man's face.

"I can manage fine with the boys. I was just worried that you might be feeling poorly . . . Miz Shields."

I had to smile at that. "Ain't likely," I told him. "I haven't felt poorly since I was a real little girl . . . Mr. Shields."

He looked at me still. "I brought you a peck of potatoes. I'll shoulder them in after a bit . . . Miz Shields."

Jim Beam couldn't stand it any longer. "Aw!" he shouted, "Aw, Pa! Can't you say her name? Say Ma! You're making it sound like she doesn't belong to us!"

I was flabbergasted! Of all of them, Jim Beam was the last one I'd ever expect to have said that.

The man's eyes twinkled, he sipped his coffee, "Can't do that, son. She's not my Ma!"

Jim Beam was nothing if not practical, "Then we have to give her a name so you can call her by it. She's my Ma, and I don't like that Miz Shields!"

Beth turned great big eyes on me, "Haven't you got a name, Ma?" She gawked in awe.

"Sure, I've got a perfectly good name."

Beth stared a minute longer.

"Don't care!" screeched Jim Beam. "I can do better! Named ol' Hog, didn't I? Didn't I? I can name you too, Ma! I can do it best!"

"I remember!" Beth squealed, "I remember! You told old Miz Colbey, didn't you?" I nodded at her. "It's Lucy!" she burst out.

"Aw!" Jim Beam was disappointed. "I can do better! How about "Tildy? Ma? I like Tildy! Pa, say Tildy!"

The man leaned back on his stool and looked at Jim Beam. He was smiling. "Why, I reckon Tildy's right pretty, Jim Beam," he drawled, "but Lucy's right pretty, too. Guess I'll have to call her Lucy because that's her name."

He took the boys outside with him. I strained the pail I'd got at the morning's milking, but hanging it down the well would have to wait. I'd have to draw a lot of water that morning.

But when I went outside, the man had already toted the water. The full boiler sat on its rocks over a fire and the steam was already wafting up. The wash tub sat on the bench half full of cold water.

This was a good chance. I scatted Beth up the ladder and across that wobbly plank to push the boy's bedding down. I was right. It was a real rat's nest! So I split my time. I boiled a tub, and I soaked a tub while I spaded, turning the ground and then hoed the rows.

Beth dropped seed and covered while I rubbed out a tub of clothes and hung them. And by repeating the process, we got both chores done.

Beth looked at the pictures on the little packets of seeds. "Why do we have to plant the turnips and onions first?" she asked. "The beans are prettier."

"Because," I explained, "things that grow under the ground like potatoes and turnips and onions have to be planted in the dark of the moon. That's now. Things that grow on top of the ground, like the beans and cabbages, do best if they're planted in the light of the moon. Two, three days from now we'll plant the beans and the others. Today we do the turnips and onions. And the wash!"

I had to tighten the rope and string more if I wanted Jim Beam and Fly's bedding dry come sunset. I got some extra spading done, but that would just make it easier next time.

The sun was high overhead by the time we were finished. It was dinnertime, and I reckoned the menfolks were good and hungry. I made the bottom of the big pot full of biscuit. It worked right well for an oven. I fried slabs of venison, cut a little raw for Lost Be, cut the biscuit and put the meat inside, while I fried a skillet full of potatoes. I packed the hot food in a pail, hung the milk down the well and took the water pail and dipper. Beth and I set off for the field and sat on the ground with our menfolk to eat.

Jim Beam flung himself down and took a mammoth bite of the bread and meat.

He chewed and swallowed. "Crimme! I'm hungry! Guess ain't no boy has ever been no hongrier than me! Guess I could eat a buffalo! A whole buffalo!"

I laughed at him. "Well, we haven't got a buffalo," I told him, "but, we've got some potatoes."

"That's for me!" he yelled, "A lot of potatoes for me, Ma!" So, I gave him "a lot of potatoes" and I dished them up for the rest of us.

I wished that I'd had some eggs to hard-boil, but I didn't. I wouldn't neither until Biddy hatched out her chicks and the pullets got big enough to lay. But it was nice and kind of like a picnic. We ate every bite of food.

We worked the rest of the day and we got a lot done. At sunset, the man squinted at the sky and started to unhitch the horse. There'd be no rain tonight; he was fixing to leave the plow in the field. I stopped him. "Reckon you ought?" I asked, "Tomorrow is the Sabbath."

He stared at me, but he didn't say anything. He just buckled the strap back, turned the plow, and drove the horse in.

I fixed for Biddy and Hog and the man, and the boys fed them while Beth fed Lost Be. The man took the pail out of my hand, "I'll milk."

"I plan to teach Beth as soon as I get to it." He nodded and went out.

After we ate and washed up, I stood on the floor and handed the clean bedding up to Fly on the ladder while Jim Beam stomped back and forth across the plank carrying it to the cubby.

"You ruined it!" he shouted down at me, "I had it fixed just right! You done ruined it, you did! I'll never get it fixed right again. Not never, Ma! How come you went and done that? Huh?"

I let him holler. If it wasn't that, it'd be something else. Just wait a bit. I reckoned he'd holler more.

I made the boys fill the boiler and build a fire under it, and I fetched the wash tub into the pantry with a couple of buckets of cold water in it.

Beth clung against my skirts. "What are you going to do, Ma?" she whispered.

"It's Saturday night," I explained. "That's bath night."

"Bath!" she gasped, "Everybody?"

"Every single one!" I was positive.

She purely goggled at me. "Pa won't like it," she warned.
"Oh! I suspect he will."

Don't know if he did or he didn't, but he bathed first. He even helped to carry the water. Jim Beam's mouth gaped and he stared in utter disbelief. It was well that I made the boys wait until last. I used my water for Beth first and then me. Then Fly and Jim Beam were shut together in the pantry with a clean tub of water.

We could hear them squealing and hollering and splashing. I let them play. They'd worked hard and they deserved it. I expected the floor to be muddy for a day or two, and it sure was.

I took up my knitting and Beth leaned against my knee and stared dreaming into the fire while she petted the sleeping Lost Be.

The man crossed his arms on the table and stared at me. "I have to say, *'Thank you,'* Lucy."

I tried not to jerk, "What for, Mr. Shields?"

"For doing what you've been doing." He was serious. "For coming here. For marrying me. For caring for the young'uns. For being a mother to them and teaching them. For working to help make this place into something. For all of that, and for not asking any questions."

I didn't dare to look at him. His thanks boiled down to just one thing. He was thanking me for being a woman. For being me! It gave me a start. My brothers wouldn't thank their wives!

They expected, demanded as much or more, than I had given. It was a woman's duty.

I thought of the way we had married. "Get down from the coach, Miss Blake. Say howdy, Miss Blake. Say your vows, Miss Blake. Get into the wagon, Miz Shields." And all those miles home without hardly so much as a word. It was what I had expected. And I had done only what I had expected to do—my duty.

It unnerved me some, his thanking me. I spoke right out, "It's no more than any woman could do, Mr. Shields. You have given me a home of my own, and a family and . . . ," I hardly dared say it, ". . . and a man of my own."

I waited.

"It seems to me you're doing a lot." He cleared his throat, "I reckon I'm not used to it. Nor the young'uns neither."

My eyes flew up. "But, their mother? Jim Beam's mother, your wife. Didn't she . . . ," I broke off sharply.

"Lizbeth was always poorly . . . health wise. She couldn't make the effort to do much. It wasn't her fault! She should never have been brought out here."

He was blaming himself. No use to that. I changed the subject. "You never made the boys help her?"

He sighed, "I didn't rightly know how."

A man that didn't know how to teach and guide his own young'uns? I didn't say anything.

It wasn't my place to take him to task.

He sat a while longer and then he got up. "I'm going out to take a look around," he muttered, "you'd best bar the door."

That meant he was going out by himself for a while before he bedded down . . . in the barn.

I thought over what he'd said.

Did Lizbeth's being *so poorly* explain Fly? Maybe. But then, Fly was a good year older than Jim Beam. Lizbeth had born Jim Beam and later Beth. Could be she was just poorly sort of, off and on.

I left the boys' bath water set in the muddy pantry floor. It would keep until morning and no harm done.

After chores and breakfast the next morning, we all gathered around the table and I read out of my bible. I didn't figure they'd had much bible reading, so I read the Twenty-ninth Psalm. Then we bowed our heads and we said the Lord's Prayer. That is, I said it a line at a time, and they repeated it. All except Fly. I didn't hear him say one single word.

After dinner, the man and the boys disappeared. It must have taken some time to notice.

"Where did they go?" I asked Beth.

She wrinkled her nose and squiggled, "I reckon they went fishing."

"Fishing!" I stared while she kissed Lost Be square on the nose.

"I reckon. Pa's always promising Jim Beam, but they never had time afore."

"Where?" I demanded.

She prodded Lost Be's soft little stomach with her bare toes. "Where what?" she didn't look at me.

Now I knew she was quicker than that! "You know right well!"

"You won't be mad, Ma?"

I relaxed. Jim Beam wasn't going to get cheated out of his fishing trip by me. "Of course I'm not mad," I told her. "I just thought we might get some good watercress near a river. It's good eating greens, but I suppose we could just as well get it tomorrow. Today we could just as well go out in the woods a bit and find some more poke greens. Might be we'll pick a little extra for Hog and Biddy."

She grinned, "Hey, Ma, you just know everything, don't you?"

No, I didn't know everything, but I was learning. She was showing me, and so was Jim Beam and Fly and, yes, even the man. They all needed me. Yes, they did. And they were open in their gratitude. They made me need them. But all their needs were different. I must broaden myself, spread out to meet these needs, just like Biddy spread out to take my pheasant eggs under her.

We went to the woods, Beth and me. I found the poke greens and picked my apron full. Beth picked hers full of sparse, kind of wilted wild flowers. She coaxed Lost Be after us and the pup wallowed in the fresh grass and nipped at our heels.

I didn't say Beth nay, because the soul has got to live or it doesn't do the body any good to breathe. I always tried to teach Beth the basic needs of life, but I always tried equally hard not to wound that wonderful special inner core she possessed.

It was strange. I had seven brothers and they had young'uns by the score, and yet, I had never crossed any such as these. Beth, Jim Beam, and Fly.

I had been lucky. God had watched me. Only here could I have found these children. Only here could I have found this man.

We fixed potatoes to bake and boiled off the poke greens, leaving some for Hog and Biddy in the pan.

"Sis-s-s-t!" I cautioned Beth, "We'll not make any meat until we see if they catch some fish."

She squiggled again and hugged Lost Be and she set the table.

They did. The man filled the wash tub with cold water for cleaning and I was there with a pan to take the waste for

Hog. "Just the fish parts," I told an over-anxious Jim Beam, "Hog doesn't want all those scales!"

Jim beam waved the fish, first head then tail as he danced, "See that big one?" he screamed.

"Pa caught it! A big ol' fish pulled Fly right in the river! I caught three of them! I did! Didn't I, Fly? Didn't I, Pa? I caught that one and that one and that one! I did! Hey, Ma, did you ever catch three fish?"

"No, I reckon not," I assured him. "I'll bet they're just going to be awful good in the pan."

They were. I kept Beth by me while I fried and I let her serve. The menfolk ate. We ate when they were finished.

Fly stared at me in that square, flat-faced way he had. "My mother is wise," he said. "I shall tell Howl-of-the-Wolf. He will be pleased." I was learning.

"Well, thank you, Fly." The man only stared.

I took my knitting by the fire. Beth leaned her arms into my lap, "Tell the story again, Ma," she asked.

I had to think quickly. What were the stories in the book I'd just read to Buck's young'uns?

"Well now," I drawled, "I know more than one story. How about *Tom Thumb?*"

"Tom Thumb?" Beth wrinkled her nose.

"Yes," I nodded, "a little man no bigger than your thumb."

"Aw!" shouted Jim Beam, "It ain't so!"

"Of course not," I conceded, "but it's a story. Do you want me to tell it?"

Jim Beam was caught flat-footed. He stood in the middle of the floor and looked around.

No one said anything. "Yes!" he screamed, "Yes! Tell the dumb story!"

And so I told it. Beth's arms softened; she slid forward upon my knees. Fly leaned against the hearth wall, his eyes slitted. No doubt he had heard many a half-believed fairy tale.

It was Jim Beam I had to contend with. He danced and he shouted. "It ain't so!" he hollered, "that's dumb!" And he wound up shouting hoarsely, "Aw! Aw!"

I smiled as I motioned the boys above and tumbled Beth into the bed. She was lulled into dreaminess. I gave her Lost Be in her arms.

Chapter Eight

The man watched me, and when I turned from the bed, he rose from the table. "You're a fine, handsome woman, Lucy." And he was serious!

Dumfounded, I couldn't answer, and he stalked from the house. I barred the door. It took me all night to resolve his words. Yeah, he'd been a widower for some time, a year at least, I reckoned. A man and a woman alone in a place like this . . . well, I suspect maybe I was looking good to him, but he was still in love with *Lizbeth*. It didn't set well with me.

In the days that followed, we did many things. We finished the rest of the corn field. We planted one in rye and one in oats and one in alfalfa. Beth and I finished the truck garden. Jim Beam filled out his bony frame. Fly took on the graceful bend of the willow and even little Beth rounded out. But every ounce she put on only emphasized her delicate build.

Lost Be grew from the waddling, round pup size to the waddling, gangly pup size and nosed Beth's heels wherever they went. Hog grew to where we used Fly's trough and added another plank-rail to his pen. Moon Eyes butted Jim Beam familiarly in the seat of his pants every time she got the chance, and he accepted it, but never without a holler. Biddy hatched out her eggs and even all but two of the pheasant eggs. I turned them loose to peck the yard.

I got the house clean and I kept it that way. I used the pieces of goods the man had brought to make dresses for Beth and shirts for Jim Beam. When I offered to sew for Fly, letting him pick his own material, he declined.

He thrust a beautifully cured deer skin under my nose. I closed my eyes. I didn't have to ask. It was Jim Beam's deer.

Fly stared at me in the way I had become accustomed to, "My brother gives me a shirt," he stated.

"That's as it should be," I answered him.

I didn't offer to sew it. I knew he would carry the skin whole back to Howl-of-the-Wolf so that he might brag on his brother.

I shared the cloth. Dresses for Beth, shirts for Jim Beam and the man. It nagged at me that the man was more solemn and more distant than ever. I fed him well; I tended my chores and he watched me.

I fed Biddy and her chicks, calling, "Come Biddy. Here chick, chick, chick." And I scattered grain for them. He watched me, clunking the axe in the stump and standing idle while he stared.

I taught Beth to knit and kept her near. She was always at my skirt and my knee and she shyly crept into man's lap in the evening times. She loved Jim Beam with a passion that exceeded the preservation of her life, but she courted the approval of her father as a coquette. Fly, she adored, and she was sure of her reception there.

You would have thought that there had never been another woman in that house besides me. She mimicked me. She took on my ways. I had to start the "we women" talk with her much sooner than I had thought to.

I got desperate. I tried to start her on all I knew, but that wasn't enough for Beth. She craved life and she'd be satisfied with nothing less. I twisted every which way to avoid her. I could not.

In wild desperation, I followed the man out of the house one night, "Mr. Shields!"

He jerked around at me. I went as far as the well and he followed. I swallowed hard and hugged my arms across my chest, "Mr. Shields! I need to have a baby!" He gulped. I could hear him. Once it was out, there was no stopping me.

"It's time! I've done as best I could! I've tried! I feel this is my land! Those are my young'uns! Yes, even Flying Cloud! He's mine, too! And you aren't being fair, Mr. Shields!"

He was right behind me. His voice came out even. "You want a child, Lucy? My child?"

I spun about on him and I had to look up, "Yes! Yes, I do. And the sooner, the better!"

He stared down, "You know what you married don't you, Lucy?"

Yeah, I knew, or I thought I did, but . . . "I don't know anything!" I cried, "I see what I see! And I want a baby of my own."

"Do you know what you're offering?"

"I'm not *offering* anything. I'm your lawful wedded wife and you have no right to deny me! I need a child. And Beth, she . . . ," I stopped.

He clenched his hands on my shoulders, "Beth?"

I bit my tongue. I hadn't meant to let that slip out. I shook off his hands and drew myself up. "It doesn't matter. I'm asking you for a child, Mr. Shields. It's your duty!"

He stared at me hard. "Yeah," he finally spoke, "You're asking me for a baby . . . *for Beth*!"

And for me!" I cried quickly, "And for you . . . ." I shut my mouth sharply. That was the wrong way to go.

He laughed that short, bitter, unfunny laugh. "Sure! Another young'un for Roan Shields! You're going to have a long wait for that, Lucy!"

He left me with my head hung down, standing by the well.

I hated him! I hated him good, and I slapped the bolt into place with force that night. The next day, I started to teach Beth that all the things worthwhile took time. In the meantime, I stung the man when I got the chance.

On one occasion, I snapped at him, "I'm not about to die from birthing a baby! Not one and not ten!"

Another time, I taunted him, "I won't be poorly neither, not before nor after any baby!"

And finally, I faced around on him defiantly. "Mr. Shields," I told him, "You are just plain mean!"

It didn't do me any good. He bedded himself in the barn and that was that. I gave up.

There was no pushing a man that didn't want to be pushed.

In the weeks that followed, little green shoots began to shove up their heads and things began to grow. The pheasant rooster must have been in one of the eggs I'd mashed the day we'd chased Hog, because all the clumsy little brown lumps that truckled after Biddy were pullets. Out of Biddy's own fourteen eggs, I got five cockerels. I'd just keep one and picked out the one that seemed biggest and strongest.

Field crops were in and growing and now, it was up to God. Of course, we hoed the rows, all of us working in the fields and Beth and I doing the truck garden. We'd be eating it before long.

I was gratified that there was little likelihood of a water shortage what with the well and the creek. The creek was broad and fairly deep and not much chance of it drying up, even if the well did. It supported a plenty of watercress and there were still poke greens in the woods.

Jim Beam got to be a better shot. He never again took the gun on his own. Of course, he didn't ask either. He shouted his announcement that he was taking it, and then I either nodded and he took it, or I said, *"Not today, Jim Beam, you have chores to do"* and he didn't take it.

The game in the pantry began to build up faster than we could eat it, but we'd need it come winter. So, the man built a smokehouse out of what was left of the planking, with the boys helping, and he caulked it up good with the clayish mud from the creek banks. It was airtight save for the small opening in the top.

They took the horse and dragged in a good-sized limb of hickory. Well, if he was going to smoke what he could hang in there with hickory, then I wasn't going to dress out any chickens for fryers. Not even the cockerels, yet. Feeding was easier now, and it would be in the fall, all things going well, and I'd save them for stewers come winter. The pheasants too. Did the cockerel I intended to save get big enough, could be I might get another setting from Biddy before it got so cold the chicks would freeze. In that case, I'd use them for fryers and save these pullets for layers.

Wonder when pheasants get big enough to lay? I'd find out.

I looked up and the man was holding to the hickory limb with one hand, the hatchet with the other, looking at me and just standing. I went into the house.

Jim Beam and Fly got another deer. This time, Jim Beam brought back almost all the powder and shot he had taken save enough for two loads. The man fingered the powder horn, "Best to leave the gun loaded," he advised. "There's bears around now!" I jerked. He'd known it all along.

Jim Beam heralded his kill the same way he heralded everything he did, right or wrong, true or false. He shouted it to the house tops!

"Hey, Beth!" he bellowed, "Hey! Got another one! Did! Hey, didn't I, Fly? W-o-o H-oo! I did! Hey, Ma! A buck with horns this big!" He ran and leaped with his arms stuck up in the air to show how big.

I reckoned from his carryings on, the deer's antlers had to be at least twenty feet wide. Glad he was showing me in the yard and not in the house.

"They're called antlers," I told him.

"Huh?' he stopped dead still, but only for a split second, "Aw!" he shouted, "Horns are horns, ain't they, Pa? Hey, Fly! Ain't they? Don't care! They're that big! Woo-Hoo-Eeeee! I'm gonna put them in the cubby! I am! Sure! Hey, Fly, ain't we?"

I looked at the man. I couldn't see why he just kept standing there looking at me and made me teach Jim Beam everything. It kind of put me out of patience, it did, and made me snap sharply at Jim Beam, "No, you're not!"

Then he did dance and scream. "Aw! Am too! How come I can't? They're mine! Hey, Fly! Hey, Pa! Ain't they? How come I can't do it, Ma? Hey! How come?"

"I am not having no deer's horns that big hanging up over my head whilst I'm sleeping in my bed, Jim Beam. Just don't get cart before the horse. Let's wait until the deer is brung in and butchered out and then we'll see about the antlers."

And that was the way it was done. They toted in the deer, skinned him out and cut him up, and he was hung in the smoke house. The man took one chunk and, whetting the great knife, he sliced it nearly paper thin. I thought I knew what he was doing. The Indians did that and when the thin strips were smoked, they could be carried in a pouch to eat on a trip. That this was intended for Flying Cloud's trip back to Howl-of-the-Wolf, I did not know.

About Jim Beam's antlers: they were six-pointers and not nearly a yard wide. The man fixed them and set them against the chimney over the mantle. Jim Beam stared in awe, and when the man cradled the gun across the two lower prongs, his face lit up.

"Hey!" he shouted, "That's the best! I knew it was gonna be! Hey, ol' deer horns! Hey, ol' gun!"

Fly cured this skin, too. But this time he brought it to me. "It is for you, my mother. I will show you how to make moccasins for my brother and sister so that they will have warm coverings for their feet when it grows cold and the snows come."

And so, I worked with Fly fetching out my biggest darning needle and threading it with the strong thin strips of buckskin that he cut for me. I punched holes with the awl and stitched carefully.

And at last, with thanks to Fly, both Jim Beam and Beth were shod.

I finished the socks I had started for the man and I knit a pair for Beth and for Jim Beam. The socks with the moccasins would indeed keep their feet warm this winter. And I knit a pair for Howl-of-the-Wolf! These I kept from all eyes save my own for I was a little ashamed of every row I knit. They sure were shameful! The toes were red, the heels purple and I used every color yarn I owned in between. Blue, green, yellow and pink, but I worked a methodical pattern.

When I folded them away in my trunk, I was doubtful I'd ever be able to lift them out again. That's how awful they were. How Buck would have laughed if he'd seen them.

We began to eat from the truck patch. They savored the tiny scallions I thinned from the patch, and when I stewed some of the first tomatoes, Beth squiggled in ecstasy. She put her arms around my neck that night in the big bed.

"Hey, Ma," she whispered, "you are just the best Ma there ever was!"

Jim Beam was different. I don't know, but I guess he had need to be. When I pulled and pared and boiled off the first turnips, he gobbled them down and then turned startled eyes on me.

"What was that?" he demanded loudly.

"Those are turnips" I announced smugly.

"Turnips!" he shouted, "I don't like 'em! I don't want no more turnips, never! Don't like 'em! Ain't never gonna like 'em! I'd sooner have pie! Hey, Ma! Can't you make turnips pie?"

I smiled. Poor Jim Beam. He'd only known raisin pie and he figured all pie would taste like raisin, even if it was turnip.

"Well," I drawled at him, "there's some people who have to learn to like turnips. You'll get used to 'em, Jim Beam."

"Naw!" he screamed, "Never! Unless they're in a pie!"

So, that night I boiled off a little molasses taffy. Standing at the table, I pulled it until it cooled a little and turned a pretty color. Then I showed them to dip their fingers into a pan of sugar and pull their own. I twisted off bits and handed them out. Not too much, because I didn't expect most of theirs to get pulled. I knew they would take bites and not much would get hard enough to get cut up.

Jim Beam was first, as I had expected. He investigated everything new. He took a great bite out of his palm. His eyes got great big and he chewed and pulled frantically. He swallowed.

"What's that?" He shouted.

"It's candy" I pulled away. "It's for Christmas time and birthdays, and special celebrations. It's a lot more special than pie."

"Whoo-Hoo-Eeeee! Ain't it just!" he shouted, "Candy! Hey, Beth! Ain't it good? Hey, Ma! What's Christmas?" I pulled a nub onto a fingertip and popped it into Beth's mouth. That was all she needed. Of course, she only had a small piece. It was all her tiny hands could handle. She nibbled around the edges and squiggled for as long as it lasted. Even Fly could not resist.

With his first mouthful, he looked at me and he didn't need to say anything.

The man dipped into the sugar pan and came around the table to me and we pulled together. It was a happy, warm time and the young'uns went to bed more content than they ever had. I don't think it was the candy. It was doing something together and seeing me and the man doing something together. It made a wonderful warmness. Or, maybe, it was the spirit of Christmas in the middle of summer. I told them the story of Christmas. Maybe I laid a little heavy on the biblical story and a little easy on the Santa Claus and presents. I wasn't sure how we'd be fixed come Christmas and I didn't want them to be disappointed.

I cuddled Beth when I went to bed. What kind of a life had they had that they didn't even know about Christmas?

CHAPTER NINE

The man and the boys cut and peeled willow and put a corn crib against one of the barn walls. Come corn shucking time I'd show Beth to split and plait the shucks into straw hats for the men. Come next summer the sun wouldn't beat on everybody's head.

I began to hold back on the goats' milk and set it for cheese. I got several makes, and while they were small blocks, they were food, and every little bit counted. I canned out of my truck patch, putting down whatever I could, in any kind of containers I could find. Beth helped with a will and she was quick.

The menfolk fished and put their catch down in salt in a barrel. They smoked the meat from hunting in the smokehouse.

And then came the day when it was time for me to take Moon Eyes on a lead rope back to the Colbey's billy. That was a trip I didn't want to make. But, there again, first things first. We needed Moon Eyes' milk. Didn't matter that, somehow, I didn't like the Colbeys.

I jumped Beth up as best I could, and I pulled the locket out onto the front of her dress. I dressed myself and away we went with Moon Eyes baa-ing on the end of the lead rope, and Lost Be nipping at her heels.

I was surprised at first by the welcome I got. Miz Colbey pushed me to come in for a cup of tea while Mr. Colbey saw to putting Moon Eyes with their billy. I touched the bit of gold in my pocket. Maybe I'd keep the kid this time. Pray God, it was a billy and the next one a nanny.

I didn't like sitting in Miz Colbey's house and I didn't like drinking her tea. I didn't like answering her questions either. Next neighbors or no next neighbors, I didn't like nobody butting their noses into my business. I especially didn't like Miz Colbey doing it. I pulled Beth against my knee.

The Colbey house might be plank on the outside and white washed, too, but inside it was no bigger than the Square Heap. There was only one window and the hearth was stingy little. The floor was puncheon and it was sure good and dirty. Her man hadn't done nearly as well by her table and chairs and stools as mine had. I stuck my chin up a little.

She poured tea into tin cups and eyed me sideways, "How are ya' likin' it around here by now, Miz Shields?"

"Right fine," I told her.

"Ya' sure do have a passel of young'uns over to yer place."

"Some," I wondered what she was getting at. She knew as well as I did that there were young'uns at the Square.

"Reckon there's gonna be more soon, Miz Shields?" This time her tone was sly. That made me tired! Why didn't she just come out and ask plain-like, was I going to have a baby?

"God willing, Miz Colbey." I sure wasn't going to tell her anything.

Guess she didn't like my answers, because she laughed shortly, "Heared tell that warn't needed with Roan Shields. He done proved his worth."

Now, she should have known better than that! I faced her down square, but I wasn't going to lose my manners, "You don't have any children, Miz Colbey?" I asked sweetly.

Her face went kind of slack. "I ain't never been a well woman." She didn't look at me, "Takes all my strength just to keep this place a-goin'."

That was a lie if ever I heard one. But then, of course, she wasn't going to tell me her man was no good. I started to pity her.

"I see your crops are coming along," I offered.

She took hold again, "Yeah. They're doin' right well. My ol' man reckons to be needing some help right soon. It's hard for one man to be a-doin' ever'thin' on a place."

She sure was slickery. Why didn't she say what she meant? I knew what was coming, did she ever get around to it, and I stiffened.

"Yes, I suppose," I agreed and waited.

"Miz Shields, we been a-thinkin' on it, my ol' man and me has, and we reckoned we could take one of the boys off'n yer hands. What with my ol' man needin' the help and. . . well, it wouldn't be like he was a bound boy or nothin' like that. We'd care for him just like he was our own. He could sleep in the barn, and I'd feed him good twice a day. What do you say, Miz Shields? We'll take one of those boys off'n yer hands?"

Well, there it was. She couldn't get no young'uns of her own, and likely none of anyone else's neither, so she was after a Roan Shields woods colt! Did she reckon I was a lazy slattern like her own-self, that'd be glad to palm off the young'uns because they weren't my own flesh and blood? Or did she reckon I'd break down and complain to her of my lot and the man I'd married?

I didn't really know what she expected, but it sure wasn't what she got.

Beth was staring. I squeezed her hand. "Why, thank you kindly, Miz Colbey. I reckon it was right neighborly of you to think of us. But we haven't got any boys to spare. No siree. Not a-one. Nor girls either. I don't reckon you've seen the Square lately, Miz Colbey. We've been awfully busy over there putting up and laying by for the winter. I thank you, but we need to have all our young'uns at home with us."

Her face kind of soured up. "Well, I . . . *we* were only lookin' to help you out," she muttered.

Mister Colbey saved me from having to answer. He came in and sat down to the table sort of like his bones collapsed. "Wal', I put yer goat in with Billy, but I reckon ya' oughta leave her a day or so. Just to make sure, ya' knows." He grinned a slightly nasty grin.

I sure didn't like the Colbeys! I didn't like leaving Moon Eyes, neither. I got up, straightened my skirt and took Beth's hand, "Then I'd best be getting back."

I was real polite, "Thank you for the tea, Miz Colbey. You should walk over to the Square one of these days. Mister Colbey, I'll be coming back tomorrow for Moon Eyes."

He looked at his wife and she nodded at him. "Why, reckon we could save you the walk, Miz Shields. I ain't seen Roan Shields' place in years. Might just be we could lead your goat home tomorrow."

I hadn't thought to have my invite taken up so quickly. But it didn't matter. They wouldn't be satisfied until they'd seen what was going on at the Square, and if I hadn't asked them, they'd have come anyhow. This way, it was getting it over with quick-like. "Oh I don't want to put you to any trouble, Mister Colbey."

"No trouble. No trouble a-tall!" his wife put in.

"Why then, I'd be right obliged."

"Perfectly aw-right," he sputtered, "perfectly aw-right."

I touched the gold in my pocket. Sure, a kid oughtn't to cost any more than a pup. "And one more thing, Mister Colbey," I held the coin out to him, "We want to keep the kid this first time and I'm offering you this as payment, if you agree."

Miz Colbey grabbed his hand. "Wal'," she made it slow, "I don't know . . . a kid . . . ."

I put the money back in my pocket. "Oh, alright, if you need the kid . . . ."

Mr. Colbey burst in, "Now, now, Miz Shields. Come, Alice, we can spare the kid. After all, they's our next neighbors."

I put the coin on the table, "Then good morning to you both." I had some trouble being polite that time, "We'll be watching for you tomorrow with Moon Eyes."

They followed us outside and Beth whistled up Lost Be. Once through the gate, I took a good long breath of fresh air. Imagine her offering one of our young'uns a bed in the barn and two miserable meals a day! It took me all the way home to get over my mad.

They did just what I hoped they would do. They showed up leading Moon Eyes, and just in time for dinner. I reckon it was mean of me, but I sure got my satisfaction from that visit.

We showed them clean, well-fed, well-dressed, well-be-haved young'uns. We showed them a well-kept, good-run-ning farm and I showed them a clean house and a full larder, plus I served them a meal I'd have been proud to serve to anybody. I tried to have the things I thought they wouldn't be used to. I guess I managed right well, because Miz Colbey's mouth got tighter and tighter while her husband's got bigger and bigger.

My man didn't say much, and when he did, he talked strictly about the farm. He was quiet and easy and I was proud of him, too.

They didn't stay long, and I couldn't help smiling as I watched them walk away. I didn't expect they'd be coming back again soon. I was plum self-satisfied by what we had. We'd worked hard to get it, but we were beginning to reap the fruits of our labors. I knew from Beth that there had been no animals, except the horse, on the farm since she could remember, and I didn't know the how come of that. Roan Shields was a good farmer. You could tell by the way his fields looked now and I guessed that he'd had good crops before this. I gathered from Beth that her mother had been dead more than a year when I had come. That meant just one thing. The empty larder, the lack of clothing, and all else save the barest necessities was due to the fact that it had taken every cent Roan Shields could scrape together to pay Burtram Thompson for the advertisement, his work, and my passage.

I wished my dowry had been twice as much. And Buck could have added some to it, if Becky wasn't so mean. Well, no matter. Things were looking up now and we'd make out just fine on our own.

Two days later, Fly came to the breakfast table with his deer skin made into a roll and tied with a thong. A small pouch hung at his side. The man looked at him a long time, "Do you have to go, Fly?"

The boy nodded solemnly, "Howl-of-the-Wolf will expect me in his lodge by the next full moon. I must go now."

The man nodded back, "You take that pemmican, Fly. And stop at the barn. I've got some tobacco fer Howl-of-the-Wolf."

Fly smiled. It was the first time I'd ever seen him do it and it made me tremble. His mother must have been very beautiful.

Red-cheeked, I brought out the awful socks. Beth clasped her hands and breathed, "Oh, ain't they pretty!" and Jim Beam gave a long, loud "Whoo-Hoo-Eeeee!" But Fly thanked me so earnestly I got all flustered.

I put my arm about his shoulders, "We'll look for you to be back by winter, Fly."

He followed the man out. Beth watched him go with great big eyes, but Jim Beam dashed out the door and around behind the house and didn't come back until dinnertime.

Flying Cloud didn't talk very much, but it seemed awful strange and quiet without him. We all missed him a great deal, but Jim Beam really suffered. He was lonesome, no doubt about it, for he made Beth's life miserable. I showed him how to make a willow whistle and a fluttermill, but I finally had to blister his bottom again before he got over pouting.

For me, Fly's going left a gap that was hard to get used to. Weeks after he was gone, I found myself cooking more than we needed and half a dozen times a day I caught myself turning about with his name on my lips.

And then I made up my mind. It was getting on towards the end of summer. We were doing catch up work. I was putting up what we couldn't eat of my truck garden. My rooster, named "The Croaker" by Jim Beam, because of his raucous, immature crow, was half grown, but the pullets wouldn't lay until the new year. We'd eaten the other four cockerels, so The Croaker was really the cock of the barnyard.

Moon Eyes wasn't showing her kid yet, but my blocks of cheese were growing in number. The corn ears were putting out wisps of silk and the man was leaving time to walk the waist-high fields of grain.

He cut saplings from the woods and dragged them in and spent some time every day chopping wood, building up the wood pile. He built a rail pen for Moon Eyes inside the barn next to Horse's stall, but we still staked her out during the days.

Then he began to build the outside shutters for the Square Heap. One morning, when Jim Beam had gone to stake out Moon Eyes and Beth, with the gangling Lost Be at her heels, had followed, I turned on the man.

"Now then, Mr. Shields. I asked you once before, and I'm asking you again. I want a child, Mr. Shields."

He answered quickly, shortly, "I told you no once, Lucy."

"And you mean it?"

He nodded without words. I turned on my heel and went into the house and I fetched out a chair. I set it down and scrounged it around good, so it'd set steady, and I set myself down in it.

He looked at me like I'd lost my wits. "What are you doing?" He sounded kind of funny.

I folded my arms, and I stared him straight in the eye, "I'm not moving, not one inch, until you agree, Mr. Shields. I know my rights!"

He turned away and he was jerking and shaking something awful. When he turned back his eyes were wet and the lines deeper in his face. He'd been laughing! Well! He'd laugh out of the other side of his face when he got hungry!

He tried to soothe me, "Now, Lucy. You don't want to do this. It's going to get awful hot out here. You really don't want to do this."

"You heard me, Mr. Shields," I snapped, "I'm not moving until I know there's going be another young'un here!"

He argued a little more, but I didn't even look at him, so he finally went off, shaking his head.

He didn't come near me again. Beth ran up, propped her elbows in my lap, and stared up into my face, "What are you doing, Ma?" she asked quizzically.

"I'm sitting" I told her glumly. "You run off now, Beth, and pick some poke greens er even some flowers."

She did, but she stopped to look back at me. Then I had Jim Beam to contend with. He leaped up and walked along the top board of Hog's pen, his arms flailing wildly.

"Hey, Ma! Look at me! Ain't this something? Hey, Ma! What're you doing? You sure look dumb, Ma! Whoo-Hoo! Sure do! Hey, Ma! Ain't you getting' hot?"

I crossed my fingers. I'd smack him good if he fell and I had to get up to fish him out of the pig sty. Humph! If he did fall in, he'd get out by himself, I reckon!

Well, I sat there from a little after The Croaker's bugle until just short of dinnertime, before I was certain there was to be another young'un at the Heap. And then, it wasn't exactly what I'd been aiming at, and it came with hardly any warning.

I saw them coming, but I was just so determined that I didn't pay any attention, so the wagon pulled up in the yard nearly in front of me. It was all brightly painted with scrolls and animals, and such, like a circus wagon! The man on the seat skittered down and pulled off his tall hat. He bowed formally.

I cast my eyes around. There wasn't no one around but me, and this funny little man dressed like a drummer. I nodded at him, "How do."

He bowed again. "Madam, I am Weatherby Nottingham, proprietor and owner of the Mercurial Sulphur Stabilizing Traveling Show. You are Miz Shields, I take it?"

I got up. "I'm Miz Shields," I told him. "I suspect you must be lost. There's no one here abouts but us. Did you lose your way?"

"No, Ma'am. You are Miz Roan Shields?"

"Yes," I nodded, and I waited. How come he knew my name?

"Family down the way directed me," he explained. "Man, name of Colbey. I'm glad I've found you, Miz Shields, but you may not be as happy."

I frowned. I was put out anyway and his sashaying around didn't improve my temper. "If you have something to say, sir, say it right out. I'm in no mood for twiddle-twaddle!"

He hardly came above my shoulder and his eyes put me in mind of Hog. I didn't like him, right off. His fat jowls turned purple, "I've got this to say," he piped, "you ask Roan Shields, does he remember Marie Faberge? And you can tell him, she's dead!"

He moved quickly. He opened the door at the back of the wagon, and he dumped a sack on the ground. He scurried back up onto the seat and took up the reins. Then he looked at me once more.

"That's his whelp! *Algernon*, she called it!" he snarled. "Been carting it around these nine years and now Marie's dead, and I ain't a-gonna feed it no more! Tell it's Pa that for me!"

He laid whip to his horse and was gone before I could speak. I stared after him. What on earth? What did he mean by all that?

Well, I guess God hates a contrary woman. And Lucy Shields sitting out there in the hot sun like a durn fool sure got her come-uppance.

The bag moved. I knelt down, untied the knot, and spread the mouth. The thing inside sprang out, running like a streak. I looked up and caught sight of Jim Beam and Beth. "Catch it! Catch it!" I shrieked, and catching up my skirts, I took to my heels.

We chased it much the same way we had chased Hog. And again, it was Jim Beam who leaped and brought it to earth. And then Jim Beam did the unheard of.

"Help! Ma!" he screamed, "I can't hold him! Help!"

I leapt in, laid my hands to, and shook out what we'd been chasing. Both young'uns goggled. Jim Beam was first to his tongue. "What is it?" he yelled.

I shook it to make it hold still. "Be still!" I shouted.

I could feel it shaking in my hands, but it stopped trying to get away. Tears ran out of its eyes and it spouted gibberish in a high voice screaming wildly.

I nearly let him go in my shock. He looked like an animal. His eyes looked out like an animal, but it was a boy. Yes, it was! A little tiny, wild human boy! I didn't know what it was inside me, maybe that bit of still-wild life, that wants to hide when it is hurt, that made me take my apron up over it, head and all.

And then I rocked it and I crooned at it like you would a baby. Not with words, but just with the warmth of me.

"What is it?" yelled Jim Beam.

I shook my head at him.

Beth laid a hand on his arm. "You hush, Jim Beam," she admonished him. "You hush."

He hushed. Dinner was leavings mostly fixed by Beth because I carried my trembling burden all through it. I carried him all through the afternoon and into the evening.

It was suppertime and the man came in. I was kneeling at the hearth.

"Well, Lucy, glad to see you stirring. Thought you were going to sit out there for days."

I turned around on him. He gasped. Before he could open his mouth, I spoke sharply. "Do you remember Marie Faberge?" I demanded. "Well, a Mr. Weatherby Nottingham was by this morning. Said Marie was dead and he'd been feeding *your whelp* for nine years. This is him!"

He jerked and stared, "Marie Faberge!"

"That's what he said! And this here's your young'un, I guess."

He stared at me for a long time. "Let's see it."

"Can't," I turned a little away, "he's scared."

And so, I sat on the stool against the hearth until everyone was gone to bed. I blew out the candles, leaving only the fire light. Then I broke a little pone into some warm milk.

I turned back just the corner of my apron. I ladled the food in with a spoon.

"Algernon." I murmured, "Eat now, Algernon."

He ate like he was starved. I couldn't see nothing much below my chin, but his mouth. As long as it kept opening, I kept putting in spoonfuls of food.

I took him to bed just the way we were, with his tiny arms clenched about my neck and his head against my throat. I cuddled him between Beth and me.

CHAPTER TEN

I got up the next morning early. Algernon had turned in the night and was clinging against Beth.

I shook up the fire and lit a candle. The man came in quietly just as I was crossing to the bed. I motioned him silently.

We bent above the sleeping young'uns. Beth's face was clear and fine against the pillow, but she would never have the beauty of the face that lay against her throat. It was chiseled, perfect, and the locks of dark hair, though wild and long and dirty, were beautiful.

I met the man's startled eyes. He stretched a hand downwards and whipped away the covers. The young'uns didn't stir. Beth lay curled towards my place and he—Algernon—clasped her about the neck. His shoulders were all of as wide as Jim Beam's, yet his arms were hardly the length of Beth's. His body was nearly as long as hers, yet his ankles would have reached barely below her knees. He was naught but skin and bones.

I jerked the covers from the man's hand and whipped them back up. I flipped a small stick of kindling up into the cubby. It struck the floor and my feet within a minute. I watched, and when Jim Beam showed his head over the edge, I put my fingers to my lips and motioned him down. He came.

I took him with me to the bedside and let him look at Algernon's face. He gawked.

"Aw!" he whispered, and it was the first time I ever heard him speak below a yell, "Aw!"

"That's your brother, Algernon," I whispered at him. He gape, "Brother? Aw!"

"Yes, he is," I pulled the covers down and let him look.

He turned away to the table, "Aw!" he whispered, "Aw!"

I didn't know how to do what I wanted to do. "He hasn't been treated kind, Jim Beam," I started, "he's near been starved to death and treated badly."

"Aw! Aw, Ma!"

"You're going to have to be real easy with him for a while. I reckon the man who had him was powerful mean, because he's sure awfully afraid of everything. We'll all have to be careful until he gets used to us or he might just run away and get lost and starve to death."

"Aw!" Jim Beam whispered, "Aw, Ma! I'd find him! I would!"

"Well, we'll just have to be real careful and I reckon we won't lose him."

I shook up Beth. She squiggled and scrunched down. Algernon's eyes flew wide and before I could catch my breath he sprang from the bed and dashed across the floor. My, he was quick! He dashed frantically, first one way and then another, like a terrified, wild thing looking for a way out of a trap. At last, he wedged himself tightly into a far corner and, crouching against the floor, he put up his wee arms to cover his beautiful face. He sobbed and screamed his wild gibberish.

"He can't talk!" gasped Jim Beam.

"He acts like he's expecting a beating," I added.

The man's face was pale, his eyes looked wounded. He kept his voice down, but he trembled with rage and he cursed horribly. As a rule, I don't hold with that kind of talk, but this time I agreed whole-heartedly. Should that Weatherby Nottingham ever pass this way again, I reckoned we'd be hunting a place to hide a dead body. Right then I wouldn't think no more of killing him than I could of squashing a bug!

The man prevented Jim Beam from dashing in on Algernon. "Leave him be, Jim Beam. You'll scare him to death."

Beth crept to the table in awe and in her night gown. I didn't say anything. I was so mixed up and churning inside and I didn't know what to do. So, I just did what I always do. I cooked breakfast.

Scrunched in his corner, the little fellow gave over his screeching and sniffed and hiccoughed with dry sobs. None of us paid him any attention, though I was able to sneak a glance at him, and I saw he had lowered his arms and was peering out at us.

I dished up and sat to table, and we began to eat. "Let him calm some," I told the man, "then, I'll try to feed him."

As it turned out, that wasn't needed. We had eaten silently for a minute or two when, all of a sudden, that little one darted from his corner, snatched the pone right out of Jim Beam's hand, dashed back to his corner, and glared wildly out at us, all while he gobbled almost fast enough to choke himself.

"Hey!" yelled Jim Beam at the top of his lungs. "Hey! Ma! Did you see that! He got my pone! I don't like that!"

"Hush-t-t!" warned his Pa, "You'll scare him!"

I gave Jim Beam another piece of pone, but it, and a slab of deer meat from his plate went the same way as the first piece of pone. That was just too much for Jim Beam.

He danced in the middle of the floor and he shouted louder, it seemed, than he ever had. "Yeah! I'll scare him! The ol' pudge! Hey! I don't like that! I'll scare him and I'm gonna punch him too! Yeah! The ol' pudge! Look at my pone! I'm gonna punch him! The ol' pudge!"

To my amazement, the little one sprang up, mimicked Jim Beams frantic dancing, made awful faces, and spat and screamed his wild gibberish.

That cut it. I got up, got ahold of Jim Beam, and slapped him down on his stool.

"Sit!" I ordered.

And I got ahold of the little one too, and I slapped him down on Fly's stool.

"And you sit!" I ordered, but I held to him with one hand, while I pushed a tin plate before him. He sat and he dived in with both hands. I gave him a cup of milk and he was so eager he spilled part of it down his front.

Jim Beam was on his guard and glared at him. "Pudge!" he shouted.

The little one glared back, "Pidge!" he mimicked shrilly.

And that's how we came to have Pudge. And that, too, is how he came to be called Pudge instead of Algernon.

I looked at him. Nine years the man had said. That would put him somewhere between Beth and Jim Beam in age. His clothes were a mess of filthy rags. I made him new ones. When I saw to his first bath, there were welts on his bony back. Yeah. He'd been beaten and treated mean, but it hadn't broken his spirit. No, I reckoned they'd have to have killed Pudge to break his spirit.

No doubt, because of his size and his deformity, he had been teased and plagued by young'uns. He had grown fairly able to give back as good as he got, one way or another. He was awfully quick. All of his movements were lively, and in a foot race, he would leave Jim Beam behind like he was standing flat-footed.

It wasn't long before we came to know that, of course, he did talk. That gibberish he spouted was a language of some sort. He soon began to pick up words, and phrases, and while they had a funny-sounding twist to them, we could understand him well enough.

I had no idea how they'd raised him. Surely, he'd not been used to eating at a table, nor with anyone else. On Fly's stool, his chin barely came above the table. This did not hamper him at all. He just climbed up, stood on the stool, and leaned over the table to dip his fingers in whatever he pleased.

On the first night we had him, when he did this, I didn't reckon he should be left to get away with it. If he did it once and wasn't stopped, it would be double hard to stop him the next time. So, I cracked his knuckles with the spoon and then dished onto his plate what it was he was after.

He didn't do that anymore, but he stood on his stool and, reaching right in front of Jim Beam's shocked face, helped himself to what he wanted from his brother's plate.

The first time, Jim Beam hollered at the top of his lungs. The second time, he punched Pudge a good one.

It gave me a start. I thought Pudge would be hurt the way he went off the top of that stool.

But he balled up even as he hit the floor and bounded at once to his feet. He doubled his teensy fists and waved them while he mimicked Jim Beam's dancing and screeched his gibberish defiantly.

I turned my eyes sternly upon them. I pointed at Jim Beam and then at his stool. "You sit down, Jim Beam!" I ordered.

I made the same gesture at Pudge, and I ordered him in the same tone. They both minded. I don't know if Pudge understood my words, but he well knew what I meant. He was every bit as sharp as Beth, though there were times to come when he'd try to make believe that he wasn't.

When bedtime came, I motioned Pudge up the ladder after Jim Beam. Jim Beam stopped dead, still on the bounding plank. "I won't!" he yelled, "Ain't gonna have him for a bed-feller! Not ol' Pudge, I ain't! He's ornery! Yeah! He is!"

"He's no ornerier then you, Jim Beam!" I told him tartly, "And you just settle down. He's only about half as big as you, but he's nearly as old. Now, you don't expect him to sleep with Beth and me, do you?"

He saw the logic of that. "Well!" he shouted, "I ain't gonna like it! No, I ain't."

Pudge was in his glory. He skinned up that ladder in no time, and he ran back and forth on the plank twice. Then he crept into the cubby. In a minute, his head poked out again. I stared. He tumbled forward, head first, lit on my bed on his feet, bounced off, skittered up the ladder across the plank, and back into the cubby before I could catch my breath.

"Don't you dare!" I shrieked, "Jim Beam, don't you dare! You're too big! You'll break down my bed and I'll peg your hide to the barn wall!"

I could hear them gurgling and giggling. They sure thought they were something smart!

"You go to sleep!" I called, "I'll see to it that you'll have plenty to do tomorrow to take some of that orneriness outta the both of you."

And so, I did. I had to crack Pudge's knuckles a time or two more, but he didn't revert to snatching from Jim Beam's plate. I guess Jim Beam had cured him of that.

I watched him. Sitting on the stool he was too short. Standing on it he was too tall. He knelt down on his knees and that made him even.

I looked at the man, "I reckon he's got to have a taller stool."

He grinned. "Lucy, you are a wondrous woman."

"That doesn't make any sense, Mr. Shields," I told him primly, but I know I pinked up.

"Why, it looks to me that you always get what you want."

He could poke fun if he wanted. I didn't think it was funny. Lucy Shields sitting like a tarnation darn fool out in the hot sun! And for what? For another Roan Shields woods colt!

"Mr. Shields," I said drily, "my cup runneth over!"

He laughed. Oh, how he did laugh! Buck could never come anywhere near that roar. And it was pure laugh. Bet he hadn't laughed like that in ages. I couldn't help smiling. Jim Beam nudged Pudge with his elbow and they both laughed. They didn't know what they were laughing at. They were just laughing. Beth tittered and grinned. I reckoned it was good. A family laughing together.

I let the redding up wait a bit and Beth and me walked out with them. The man looked to my truck patch. It wasn't but half done. I'd get a lot more canning yet. I balled the cabbage heads.

Good kraut come winter. Put down in a crock with brine and spices and boiled up with some side pork or pigs' feet and knuckles. Umm, good!

I squinted my eyes. I could just hear Jim Beam. *"I don't like it!"* he'd yell, or *"I like that! Hey, Ma! Make it in a pie!"*

Bless Jim Beam. If he liked it, he thought it'd be better in a pie. If he didn't like it, he still thought it would be better in a pie.

It gave me a right good feeling way down, and I knew this was mine. Be it what it was, it was mine. I wouldn't give it up, not any part of it, woods-colts or not, for anything this side of Heaven. I wasn't even sure I'd take that into consideration. Lucy, shame on you! But I didn't have time to think about it.

Jim Beam strutted as he always did, and you'd have died to see Pudge following and mimicking him! With his short little arms and his wee bandied legs and yet, for all the world, he looked just like his brother.

Jim Beam sprang atop the fence to Hog's pen. Pudge was not to be out done.

Of course, they fell in. Both of them. I let them get out the same way they got in. Never heard of a boy falling up but I wasn't sure it couldn't happen when I saw them come out of there.

Not much worried though. Hog wasn't a razorback and not hardly big enough to do them harm. Beth's eyes twinkled. She clasped my hand, "It's nice, isn't it, Ma? Having Pudge?"

Yes. It was nice. It was nice being a family.

The man reckoned to drag more logs that day and he brought out the horse. And then we all did stare open-mouthed. Pudge ran and he sprung and he wrapped himself around Horse's front leg. He clung with a death grip and he screeched his wild jargon.

The man tried to pull him loose, but he couldn't without hurting him. Pudge screeched wildly.

Jim Beam hollered. "Put him up, Pa! Put him up!"

The man slid him up. Pudge straddled Horse's neck with his tiny legs and dug his bitty fists into the mane. He laid out along Horse's neck and sobbed out his gibberish.

Horse turned his head and looked at Pudge, but it seemed language was no barrier to him. He snorted and stamped, but he didn't seem to mind Pudge being there. I don't know what the man thought, but he started to walk the Horse, Pudge sobbing and laid out along his neck.

Without realizing it, I squeezed Beth's hand awful hard.

"What is it, Ma?" she tipped her face up, "What's wrong?"

I couldn't answer her. Pudge had not recognized me as the mother or the man as the pa. Or even Beth or Jim Beam as equals. But the old Horse, he knew! Was it possible his only friend had been a horse? Could be.

I swallowed and shook myself for Beth. "I reckon it's going to be alright, Beth," I told her. We did our regular chores, yet I couldn't help but keep an eye out. Pudge rode Horse to the barn at dinnertime. They were an uncommon long time coming in.

After we ate, I took Pudge by the hand out to my truck garden. And I led him among the rows and I pulled two fine young turnips. I put them into his tiny hands.

He stared up, tears running down his cheeks. He spouted gibberish at me.

I patted his head and motioned him away. He took off running for the stable. Now, I was sure. Pudge had lived with the horse that pulled the wagon. He had eaten with him, slept with him, and his other hours were spent tied up in the sack!

Maybe Lucy Shields hadn't been such a darn fool, setting out there in the sun after all. We had Pudge, didn't we? Right now, he loved poor old Horse. But he would love us all in time.

Yes, he would!

That night, I smacked Jim Beam good. I'm not proud of it, but I did. When I motioned the boys above, Pudge hung back. He chattered like all get out. At last, Jim Beam rolled on the floor with laughter.

"Aw!" he gasped, "He wants to take ol' Horse up in the cubby!" I snatched him up and I smacked him good.

The man caught up Pudge and, setting him atop his shoulder, carried him outdoors.

"That is not funny, Jim Beam! How would you like to eat and sleep with a horse and be tied up in a sack the rest of the time? Would you think it's as funny then?"

"Aw!" he screamed. "They didn't! Hey, Ma! They didn't! Aw, poor ol' Pudge! All tied up! Aw!"

I don't know how the man did it, but some way, he made Pudge understand that Horse had to be left in the barn and that he, Pudge, had to sleep in the cubby.

But every morning, you'd see Pudge skittering across the yard like a streak just as soon as the man opened the barn doors. And every night, the man had to take him out so that he could lay on the neck of Horse and chatter gibberish at him and pet him with his hands.

Pudge didn't make a habit out of tumbling from the cubby to my bed, but he did do it on occasion. Once, he did it before Beth was up, and he leaped on her and tickled her, laughing and chattering at her. Then he sprang away and Beth jumped up to chase him, laughing and squealing around the room. Lost Be loped after them, baying in her great big voice.

Jim Beam thrust his head over the edge of the cubby. "Hey!" he yelled, "Hey! Wait for me! Wait for me!"

I didn't wait. I opened the door and motioned Pudge outside. Beth followed, squealing, her braids flying, Lost Be galloped after them, her big, ugly ears flapping, and Jim Beam streaked by me so fast his shirt tail couldn't hit him and yelling like a banshee.

I shook my head. They made enough ruckus to be heard near to the Colbey's if not all the way. I set about getting breakfast with a smile on my face.

The man came in. It was the first time he'd caught me before I got dressed. My wrapper sure wasn't new, but it was pretty and the color was good on me. My hair still hung in the one big braid I'd plated it into the night before.

He reached out and caught its thickness in his big hand. I went awful still.

Might be I'd been going about things all wrong. I wanted young'uns and, I got to say, I'd been getting them, but it wasn't exactly what I'd had in mind. Might be there was an easier way than sitting in a chair in the sun.

He turned loose, pulling his hand away and I suddenly heard the silence. There wasn't a sound, save Lost Be's loud baying. I stepped to the door.

Our three young'uns stood together and Beth had her hand on Lost Be's neck.

Lost Be had that neck stretched out as far as it would go and she was baying at the young boy who stood not fifteen feet away.

It gave me a turn. It seemed I was always going to be a little queasy at the sight of a new young'un.

This one was tow-headed and dirty and I took it to be a boy because its bony ankles and bare feet stuck out of big cut-off britches. His white hair hung down every which way and nearly covered his eyes.

"Hey, Boy!" Jim Beam shouted, "What's your name, boy? Can't you talk, boy? Hey! What's your name?"

"Can talk!" he shouted back, "Can fight, too! What's yer own name, boy? An' what's that thing?"

That was all Jim Beam needed. He strutted forward "That's Pudge! That's what!" he shouted nearly in the other's face. "And he's my brother! And if you don't like it, I'll punch your nose! So there!"

"Aw!" hollered the other, "I don't care! I'm Toady Wooten, an' I can fight like damn hell!"

Jim Beam fell back a step, "Aw! What you said! You can't say that around here! Naw! You can't!"

The other boy bristled up. "Who says I can't?" he yelled, "I can! Can if I wants to, I can! Who says I can't?"

Toady Wooten was a bit the taller and Jim Beam might rather have had a friend than an enemy, but he wasn't going to take that.

"I'm Jim Beam Shields!" he bellowed, "And I say you can't! Hey, Beth! Hey, Pudge! Look at me! I'm gonna trounce this ol' Toady Wooten good! Yeah! I am!" Well, of course, he didn't. They squared off and stepped around some and waived their fists and shouted a lot, but nothing came of it.

I looked at the man. "Wooten?" I asked.

"Um. They've got a place up the other side of the woods. Not much of a place, reckon, got a shameful passel of young'uns."

Well, by time the young'uns had come in for breakfast, they were all fast friends and they brought Toady Wooten with them.

"Do you think your Ma would mind if you ate with us, Toady?" I asked.

"No, Ma'am, don't reckon," he gulped.

Pudge had his own high stool now, so I set Fly's for Toady between Beth and her Pa. And did he eat! Well, nobody ever ate as much as Pudge, but Toady came near it.

It was like having another of our own. Of course, we didn't bed Toady at the Square. He'd truckle off every evening in time to get home before dark, but he'd usually have supper before he left. Next morning come cock's crow, there he'd be again.

He wasn't nearly as truculent as he'd seemed that first day. Really, he was mild and easy going. He plodded along and got on well with everyone.

The man cut him a fishing pole and fixed it with line and hook when he did for Pudge. And Toady was right there to go fishing with them.

They came back with Jim Beam heralding their arrival as he always did. "Hey, Beth! Hey, Ma! Look! Look at the string Pa catched! And look at what I got! Hey, Ma! Look Toady got a pile! Hey, Toady! Didn't you? Hey, Ma! Pudge fell in! Yeah, he did! Look at Pudge's fishes!"

Pudge screeched right with him, "Pidge fishys!" he screamed, "Pidge fishys!"

Toady just grinned all over his face. They cleaned the fish and the man strung some extra on Toady's line. That day was the first that Toady went home without supper. I guessed his Ma would be glad to get the fish though.

Chapter Eleven

The weather got uncommonly hot. The truck patch had to be picked and used up or put down lest it wither on the vines. Pudge was quick as a whip at picking once he understood what he was expected to do. All the young'uns picked, Toady working right alongside Jim Beam, except Beth. She helped me with the canning. The pantry shelves were filling up. It was hot work now, but it gladdened my eye every time I looked at the lined-up jars.

The man hoed alone in the cornfields. The tassels were long and golden, and with this weather, they would soon take on the golden-brown hue just where they sprouted from the ears and then it'd be corn-shucking time. The crib would fill up, with the smaller, best eating ears left in their husks to be cleaned as we ate them and some of the bigger, tougher ones would be shucked to dry for shelling for the animals. The high sides would be put on the wagon and the rest shucked into that for hauling to the grist mill to be ground into meal.

But first of all, the very best would be picked out, shucked, dried, shelled, and put away very carefully for seed to plant come next spring.

After that, there was the scything and sheaving of the rye and oats. And then the flailing. The oats we'd barrel for us and for the animals, but again, the rye would have to be hauled to the mill.

I was thinning the potatoes now for the little new ones, but after the threshing, there would be them to dig, and I reckoned put by as best we could in straw. Might be next year we could dig a root cellar.

And besides that, there was the alfalfa hay to scythe and pitch into stacks before rain fell.

Now was the time to reap our hard work with more of the same. There would be time to rest come winter.

And so, we worked. All of us worked and those days seemed to run together. We went to bed tired and we got up tired. It may have delayed our reaping for a few days in the end, but I took time out to cook good meals. None of us could work the way we were without good food, and I didn't aim anyone should be sick just then.

We had an extra pair of hands all during this time, for Toady was constantly at our heels. He laid to with a will and worked just as hard as Jim Beam. There were days when I was sure he had spent the night in the woods. He was talling up some and he'd developed a good coat of meat on his bones. He looked good and healthy. They all looked good and healthy.

The man looked ten years younger than he had when I'd come. I don't know what I looked like because there was no time to peer into my hand mirror. I really didn't care what I looked like.

I was content as I never had been before in my life.

Sure, I was working hard, but I'd worked hard all my life. Now, I was working alongside my own man on a place that was mine with a passel of young'uns that screamed "Ma" at me. Yes, I was content.

Not that the idea of young'uns of my own had left me. Oh, no. I was still pretty determined on that point. But I decided to wait a while. I didn't aim to repeat the mistakes I'd already made on that score. Humph! Last time I demanded a young'un of Roan Shields, I'd got Pudge and practically Toady! No, I didn't reckon to make any more demands just yet.

The truck garden was finished, and we went to the corn field. We all worked together. Me and the man and Jim Beam and Toady and even Beth. Pudge perched on Horse's neck and they pulled the wagon. And so we worked the corn fields, and the stalks were all stood in shocks to dry for fodder, and the crib was full, and the man and horse hauled away a wagonful to the mill.

He was gone two days. The first day, we rested at the Square, and I was sorry the man couldn't be there. I kept Toady the night. I don't hold with keeping a young'un away from home come dark, but I reckoned Toady deserved this.

I made raisin pie for dinner. Beth squiggled for the first time in a long while. Jim Beam shouted, Pudge mimicked him, and Toady grinned from ear to ear.

After supper I boiled off some molasses taffy and we pulled it and ate it and laughed and they were happy. And I was too. I retold the story of Tom Thumb.

Because of Pudge, they all enjoyed it immensely. Pudge squealed. "Tommie!" he squeaked, "Tommie! Pidge!" And he measured the distance of his tiny thumb.

Beth threw her arms around him and kissed him soundly on the cheek. Jim Beam and Toady hooted, but Pudge didn't care. Pudge hugged Beth back, "Seestair!" he cried.

I let the boys go out to the barn and sleep in the man's bed in the hayloft.

The next day, we started scything the rye field. I swung one scythe while Jim Beam and Toady took turns with the other. Pudge and Beth sheaved and tied. I didn't push them too hard, but we'd made a good start when it was time to quit.

The man came home that night and we all stood by while he shouldered down our meal. Of course, it was not enough for Lucy Shields to look at the outside of the sacks. Not me. I opened a sack. I scooped the golden meal out and I gave a bit in their hands to each of the young'uns. I smelled it. I tasted it. I walked around the boys and I studied them. "It's the best!" I decided at last, "It's the best I ever seen!"

Jim Beam hollered. "Hey, Pa! It's best! Just the best! It's all ours, Pa!"

They all danced and squealed, "It's best! It's best!" And so it was. I was proud of it. Of us.

We reaped the rest of the rye and sheaved the oats. We took the flails, the man and me, and threshed. He hauled the rye to the mill, but he came home with an empty wagon.

"I sold the rye, Lucy," he held out the gold in his big hand.

"That's right and proper, Mr. Shields," I told him.

We threshed the oats and put them down.

Now there was nothing left but the hay. We'd have to hustle to get it in before the rain came. We hustled. Pudge drove Horse again and the barn loft was fresh and sweet and we piled a huge stack on the off side of the barn.

We were done. Crops were all in and all had been good.

"I have a hankering to go to town, Mr. Shields," I told the man.

He stared at me, "I don't like that idea much. Can't I go for you?"

"No. I don't reckon so. We're all going. I aim to take all the young'uns. I reckon you need to buy some new boots, Mr. Shields."

He grinned then, he eyed me, "You might just hear all kinds of tales, Lucy."

I let my eyes slide over the young'uns. "I reckon," I nodded.

He flushed up, "Do I have to explain it to you?" he demanded.

"I don't think so. I know what I know, and I don't put much credence in gossip."

I jumped us all up the best I could. All except Toady. He came along just as he was. I got on the wagon seat alongside the man and the young'uns piled into the back of the wagon and away we went.

The town wasn't a town, nor even a village, strictly speaking. It had two saloons, one livery, a sheriff's office and a trading post-general store. Oh, I suppose it had a forge and a gunsmith and that sort of thing, but I didn't look. That wasn't what I was after. I left the man to look after himself and Horse, and I made for the general store. All the young'uns followed me.

Because of them, I expected that I was going to get a lot of stares and maybe even comments.

But, like I said, I'm not a puny woman and I reckoned not to take too much.

The storekeeper stared, but I sailed right in, opened the big jar on the counter, and handed out to each of the young'uns a fine big peppermint stick.

"How do," the storekeeper gawked.

"How do you do," I answered polite like.

"Can I help you, Miz Shields?" he gulped.

I looked at him down my nose, "You saw that I gave all the young'uns a peppermint," I told him, "Remember that. Now. I would like to see some woolen goods for britches and I need some yarn . . . and some flannel and some pretty soft linsey-woolsey and then we'll see what else."

There was a group of men standing at the far end of the store. I paid them no mind. I figured the storekeeper's goods to be good quality. I wanted what I wanted, and I didn't reckon to go home with anything I didn't want.

A woman shouldered me. She was short and fat and didn't come up to me nowise. I shouldered her right back, but I was polite. "I beg your pardon," I told her, "I'm Miz Shields."

Her mouth gaped open, "Roan Shields' wife?"

"Why, yes," I stared at her flatly, "reckon so."

And then I looked down. She had with her two of the ugliest boys I'd ever seen. There was one near as big as Jim Beam and one a little bigger.

"You dare!" she gasped, "You dare!"

"Excuse me, Missus, but I don't know what you mean," I was quiet. Sure, I knew, but I was going to make her say it out.

"You dare to fetch Roan Shields' bas . . . ."

I stepped heavily on her foot. "These are *my* young'uns," I was real calm. "Fine-looking family, aren't they? Except for that one. He's a Wooten. But right fine looking anyway, I reckon."

She sputtered.

I looked at the young'uns. "I don't reckon I'd let my young'uns pick a fight here if I was you," I warned.

She stared.

"Hey, Ma!" yelled Jim Beam, "This here boy's teasing Pudge!"

I winked. God bless Jim Beam. He was quick enough when he needed to be.

"Hey, boy!" he yelled, "Pudge is gonna whip you good! And if he don't then I'll beat your big brother bloody! And if I can't do it, Toady here will! And if Toady don't do it, I got another brother that will! Yeah! Fly will! Yeah! Get him, Pudge! Get him!"

The men turned around. The woman moved. I caught her sharp across the shoulders.

"I reckon boys will be boys," I told her. "Now, what do you think of this wool? Would you say it was a good quality?"

I didn't have to look behind me to know. We hadn't got all the viciousness out of Pudge. And when the young one moved away, the older boy moved in. Jim Beam took up the fray. I could tell by his yelling.

"Hey!" he yelled, "Can't whip me! Not never, you dumb-bell!"

Pudge leaped against me. I caught him up. "Pidge!" he squealed, "Pidge done it!"

I patted him. "Here, storekeeper," I ordered, "give me two butterballs."

I offered them to Pudge, one at a time. "Pudge Shields," I repeated, "Pudge Shields."

"Pidge Sheels!" He shrieked happily.

The men moved in. They ringed Jim Beam and the other boy. I heard their voices. They were betting on the outcome. I leaned my elbow on the counter and I watched.

Really, it was funny. Jim Beam danced all over the other boy. He punched when he wanted and I was proud he wasn't mean with it.

"Hey, Toady! You wanna take some?" he hollered, "He ain't got nothing. Not nothing."

"Naw! You go ahead, Jim Beam!" shouted Toady.

Well, Jim Beam did go ahead. He lit in and the other boy quit.

"Hey!" It was roared from the door, and the man pushed his way to me, fairly flinging men out of his way.

"It's alright," I told him, "The boys were having a little argument about bullying." I took my arm gently away from the woman, "I don't reckon it's going to happen again."

"Demons!" the woman screeched, rushing to grab her boys, "They's demons! Look at my poor babies!"

"You had best to teach your *poor babies* not to pick on the Shields' unless they want to fight the Shields'," I told her calmly.

"You bag . . . ." she started to screech at me, but a man from the crowd interrupted her. "You best go home, Marthy."

"Willie? Why did you just stand there? Why didn't you stop 'em, Willie?"

"Th' lady's right, Marthy. Your boys started it. I don't reckon they got no more than they asked for."

I didn't pay any more attention to any of them. I bought what I wanted. The man bought his boots and paid in gold. We went home.

He pulled the wagon up in front of the Square and, at last, he opened his mouth.

"Lucy Shields! You did that on purpose!"

"Yeah," I nodded at him, "I did. I decided it might as well be gotten done and over with. I'm aiming to live here a long time."

I didn't expect to be going to town very often, but I had wanted to lay in these goods for winter work. Never did see a man could buy yard goods worth a hoot. The man's britches were wearing thin, Jim Beam's near thread-bare, and Pudge never did have a proper pair. And Beth, she couldn't go the whole winter without a flannel petticoat and a linsey-wool-sey dress for warmth.

There was buckskin left over and I'd make moccasins for Pudge.

I caught myself eyeing Toady. Poor tyke. Wondered what he was going to do come winter.

Glad I'd seen to it the man got himself a good stout pair of boots. Wondered how much money he had left. Maybe we should have gotten him a new coat, too. The one he had hanging in the barn was awful old. Well, I'd mend it up and he'd make do until next year.

We dug the potatoes. I'd try to save them to have eyes to cut come next planting time. The man fenced off a corner of the barn for Hog and he chopped an awful pile of firewood. He stacked it close to the house.

"We get blizzards now and again, Lucy," he explained. "Best to have firewood close by."

I nodded but didn't like the funny feeling I got when he said it. He'd been looking at me kind of strange-like, off and on, ever since we'd gone to town. There was sure something on his mind.

The weather changed. It cooled and it rained. At first it was a relief from the dry summer heat, but then it rained harder and harder and got colder and colder. I made Pudge moccasins and knit him some socks.

The weather didn't stop the daily coming of Toady. He still appeared every morning, rain or no rain, soaked or half-soaked, depending on how hard it was raining and all differ-ent colors of blue, depending on how cold it was. His bare feet and ankles stuck further out of his baggy britches and he still wore the same shirt as when I'd first seen him. I didn't know what to do about Toady.

And then it came around that I didn't have to do anything about Toady. Toady did it for me.

The man had taken Pudge and Jim Beam with him to the barn and Beth and I had got to our sewing when Toady came in. He was drenched, shivering, and so blue he was nearly purple. I gave him a blanket and made him go into the pantry and shuck his wet clothes. I hung them on a stool to dry and made him sit by the fire until he warmed up.

"Toady, what are you doing out on a day like this?" I asked him, "You know it's too cold to be out."

He stared at me for a long moment. "Miz Shields, can't I be your boy?"

I nearly fell off of my stool; another boy! But, at least, this time I was being asked. And this time the boy wasn't Roan Shields' child.

"Why, Toady? That's right flattering, but I don't expect your Ma and Pa could spare you."

"Why, I just reckon they could!" he flashed eagerly. "Pa says that there's too many of us and he can't make out how to feed us all this winter. Ma, she's poorly, and caring for us all is too much on her. Reckon they'd make out to spare me just fine if you would just take me in."

"Well, there's not another boy I'd rather have." I told him. "But you haven't asked your Pa and Ma, have you?"

"No, Ma'am, Miz Shields. I didn't. Reckoned I had to ask you first 'cause I know Pa and Ma'll be glad to get shed of me."

My heart ached. Poor little tad! "You just sit there, Toady, and get warm and I'll study on it. When Mr. Shields comes in for dinner, we'll ask him."

The man's eyes went wide when I put it to him. "Toady wants to come to live at the Square Heap and be our boy, Mr. Shields."

"Why, I reckon that'll be just fine whenever his Pa and Ma can spare him," he said it offhand.

I don't guess it ever crossed his mind that Toady's Ma and Pa could, and would, spare him permanently. Surely, I didn't really believe they would, neither. We sent him home that evening.

But they did, and that just goes to show, you can't always tell about people. They sent Toady back to us the next morning, lock, stock, and barrel. Also chilled through and soaking wet.

I got up out of bed to open the door to his knock, he was that early. And then I think I went back to the bed for my wrapper, because later I had it on, but I came back to stare.

The Wootens had sent us more than just Toady. He held one by each hand and I didn't have to ask anything. There were two more tousled mops of that black half curly hair and there were four great violet eyes.

Chapter Twelve

I stood there and I stared, and I thought, *we haven't got any more stools.*

Toady rushed to the hearth and shook up the fire. I took their wet dresses off. They were both boys! I put the dresses back on.

Then I shook myself. Lucy Shields, get a hold of yourself. First things first. Better get them dry some way and Toady, too. Sure like to get my hands on Toady's Ma or, might be, even his Pa!

I woke up Beth, handed her her dress, and told her to change in the pantry. I took the dresses back off the little ones and tumbled them into the bed. They snuggled down under the covers, shivering. Beth came back and I gave Toady a blanket and sent him to the pantry to get out of his wet clothes. When he came back, I sorta strung the wet things around as best I could. Then I put more wood on the fire and started breakfast. I let Toady set and get warm. His face was blue and his teeth chattered so he couldn't talk. And, of course, just like I wasn't muddled enough, the man came in. He spotted Toady right off and cocked a brow at me.

"Oh, you haven't seen anything yet," I told him tartly, "just look in the bed."

I don't know what he expected, but I never saw a man so shocked. He spun around on me, his face white and his eyes bugging out, "Where did you get them?" he gulped.

"Where did I get them? I didn't *get* them!" I snapped, "Toady brought 'em."

"Toady?" He turned on the boy.

"Yeah. I brung 'em, Mr. Shields" he admitted. "Ma said to. She can't keep 'em no more neither. She says you can have me but you have to take them, 'cause they's yours."

"Mine?" He was dumfounded.

"Yeah! Tha's what my Ma said. She said to tell you that Millie run off with a drummerman last year and now you have to take 'em."

"Millie?" He couldn't stop staring.

"Yeah. Millie. She's my sister, only lots bigger than me, and she's their Ma. Now, she's gone and Ma says you have to take 'em cause you're their pa."

He turned back and he stared at the two little boys in the bed for a long time. Then he stumped out, shaking his head, and he didn't come in to eat.

I looked at them again. They might be five, but they were puny and skinny and so most likely they were six. About a year younger than Beth. It wasn't a hard thing to figure out. An ailing wife with a new baby and a pretty, slatternly girl up in the woods. Confound such a fiddle-footed man!

I was right put out, to put it mildly, so it was just as well the man didn't come in. Not enough stools, not enough tin plates. These last three would have to go into the trundle bed and Fly was coming home soon and where would we put him? Couldn't cram three boys into that cubby!

Danged if I didn't wish I was little enough to get into the cubby. I'd just take Beth and go up there and let the whole house go to boys! You bet I would!

Jim Beam stuck his head over the edge of the cubby and peered down and Pudge tumbled out, lit on the bed, and scared himself into screaming gibberish, scaring the two little ones near to death.

I got them up and put Beth's other two dresses on them. I put breakfast on the table, and with the man's stool and mine, there were enough to go around. I ate my breakfast standing by the sideboard and that put me out some more. I got my shawl and I started for the barn.

Humph! I'd soon see to it there were enough stools, at least!

The man stared at me when I went in. He shook his head, "More Roan Shields' young'uns?"

"Well are they or aren't they?" I flashed.

"I don't know."

"You don't know, you fiddle-footed idiot?" I snapped. "And I reckon you don't know we haven't got enough stools neither? Nor plates. Nor beds, when Fly comes home. And these young'uns have no clothes and are about half starved!"

He sat down on a keg and dropped his head into his hands, "I thought you were only joking about Toady. I didn't really expect even him."

"Neither did I."

He sat a moment longer, then he got up and knocked his hand against the post and didn't look at me. "Can we make do, Lucy?"

"Well, I reckon," I said in fine scorn. "Depends on how many more of them there are. What did you think? That I was going to put them out in the snow? They're just like the other ones. We'll stretch, that's all. Only I reckon we can't stretch stools!"

I went back to the house. I gawked. Beth was just a-sizzling! She was at the sideboard standing on a stool and she was washing up. She had the two little ones a-sizzling. She handed out a pan.

"Here, Chunk," she ordered, "you take this and you wipe it good and dry and then you give it to Short. And then, Short, you take it and you set it there." She pointed under the side board.

"Here?" the little one gazed up at her in awe.

"No. Over there," she corrected him.

"Here?" he laid his hand where she pointed.

"Yes," she nodded, "Now, do it." And they did.

Jim Beam and Pudge leaped at me demanding to go to the barn. I let them go, but I had to keep Toady sitting in his blanket until his clothes got dry, which they didn't before dinnertime.

They came in from the barn and the man carried three more stools. Of course, he couldn't make a plate, so we'd have to manage. I put the twins to eating out of the same tin plate. They got along just fine that way.

"They're used to it," Toady said off-handedly, "they're always together."

I brought out what was left of the buckskin and I cut Toady a pair of moccasins. I set Jim Beam to punching the holes and I took up my needle and began to sew. Pudge watched for a while and then he pushed his little hands in my face. "Pidge done heet!" he screeched, "Pidge done heet!"

I gave over and sure enough, he worked as well as I did. He was awfully pleased and kept looking up to babble his gibberish at us all, and to screech, "See! Pidge done heet!"

And then he would boom out his deep little laugh. All of the young'uns smiled when Pudge laughed.

I set Beth to knitting as fast as her little hands could and I knit too, and Toady's long, purple feet were encased in socks and moccasins by bedtime. He paraded up and down the dirt floor glowing with pride. He clapped Pudge on the shoulder so hard he nearly knocked him off his feet.

"Thankee, Pudge! Thankee, Ma! Thankee, Beth!" he spouted in one breath, "I'm going to like being your boy! Never had no shoes afore! Never did! Hey, Jim Beam! Ain't they just monstrous?"

Jim Beam danced and shouted. "Yeah!" he yelled, "They're monstrous! Awful monstrous! Why, ain't they, Pudge? Ain't they, Beth? Yeah!"

Well, they were pretty monstrous. Toady had the biggest feet! And I bet this was first time they'd ever been warm in winter. I was glad it was done. Now, Toady could get out to the barn with Jim Beam and Pudge.

The twins would take time. They had to be started at the skin and worked out. But better they should be kept in the house than Toady. I put Beth to knitting socks for them while I cut and sewed. Silently, I thanked that woman, that "Marthy" in the store who had put me out because, in my anger, I'd bought extra cloth. Boys they were, and they were gonna have britches and shirts. All the other work went by the board so far as Beth and I were concerned, except the cooking and the redding up afterwards.

I blessed Toady, for the first morning after he got his moccasins and socks, he carried me a pail of milk from the barn. And he milked morning and night for me every day after than until Moon Eyes went dry. Because of Toady, I found a few extra minutes a day of time. I used it well.

I put him and the two little ones in the trundle. They did just fine.

In those days, when I worked so hard to clothe these last two young'uns, the man worked constantly in the barn. He came in for meals, but that was all, he didn't linger.

Beth was in her glory. She mothered those twins and they ate up the attention. They adored her. And she them. She sat flat upon the hearth and worked her knitting needles and pursed her lips like I know I sometimes did.

"It's nice, ain't it, Ma?" She asked, "I like it. Having them all here. All."

I looked at her. Delicate little Beth. I'd sure see to it that she wasn't treated by her brothers as I had been.

The twins were wild, like Toady, and the first little while they didn't say four words apiece a day. But they were Shields' too. Always they kept close together and they touched each other for reassurance. But they fought. Oh, sure they did. They fought each other and then back-to-back they fought everyone else.

The weather dried up. There was no more rain, no mud, but it was cold. Awful cold. Toady was doing the milking and caring for Moon Eyes. Jim Beam took Hog and slopped him and saw to him. Pudge, naturally, took Horse, and he was amazingly adept at caring for him. I let the little ones take care of Biddy and her brood. They scattered for them and showed me empty hands when they came in. No eggs. I didn't tell them there wouldn't be any for a while. Let it be a surprise when they found one.

On this one day, just before supper, I went to the well. Beth was standing in the door watching me and Lost Be was dashing first this way and then that, with her hackles up, baying at the top of her voice and not stirring up a thing.

Chunk and Short came out of the barn and they were scurrying because of the cold. They must have been halfway to me before it happened. They stopped. Their heads were together for a minute, then they reared back from each other.

"Can't say that!" shouted one, "I ain't a-gonna take it!" And he walloped the other a smack in the face.

The other got up, shook his head, and squared away. "Alright! You just remember you made me!" And . . . thunk! He whacked the other.

Pudge came out of the barn. I watched him. This was one of the times he tried to play dumb. He just stood there. Jim Beam and Toady passed him.

"Hey!" Jim Beam pulled up short, "Look at that, Toady! They're fighting. Sure! Hey, Toady! They can't do that! Stop 'em! Pa won't like it!"

He dashed in headlong. Toady danced and shouted behind him. "Leave 'em be!" he yelled, "Jim Beam, leave 'em be!"

But Jim Beam dashed in where angels would fear to tread and he got himself some good hard lumps for his trouble. The twins swiveled and they backed each other as though they were stuck together. Jim Beam couldn't come out on top no way at all. He ran into a flutter-mill of fists and feet but, at last, he whirled out of there and he made tracks for several yards before he stopped.

He ran his hand around his well-knocked head. "Hey!" he shouted, "Look at that! They're sure ornery! Toady why didn't you tell me? Just ornery! Leave 'em to fight! I don't care! Let them punch their own heads! I don't care! I ain't gonna stop 'em no more! Not never, I ain't." Of course, I didn't put him in mind of the fact that he hadn't stopped them this time because after another swing or two, they stopped of their own accord and took off running for the house. When I carried the water in, they were setting on their own stools at the table and butter wouldn't have melted in their mouths.

And that's the way they were. They fought regularly, at least once a day, and sometimes more. But they seldom tangled with any of the other young'uns. They punched each other about, but not much harm was done, so I just let them squabble it out. Then, when they weren't fighting, they were so good they almost weren't natural. So, I figured a little ordinary boy meanness wouldn't hurt them.

I don't know which one started the arguments, because I never did get to where I could tell them apart. Actually, I reckon Beth was the only one who could. It didn't especially matter which was which, they were so exactly alike. Leastwise, it didn't matter to me and it didn't seem to matter to them. When I called one of their names, one of them stepped out, and don't reckon there was any difference whether it was Chunk or Short.

And then, one day, the man came in between meals. The boys were all in the barn and he must have bid them stay there, because they didn't come in. There was only me and Beth in the Square and she sat, quiet as a mouse on the hearth.

He opened the door back and said, "Lucy," and I knew he was going to tell me whatever was on his mind.

He did and he sure wasn't easy about it, because he didn't lolly-gag none at all. I frowned.

I could see the way he put it that it made sense, but I sure didn't cotton to the idea.

"You really think that's best, Mr. Shields?" I demanded.

He looked at me kinda tired-like. "I don't know that it's best, Lucy, but there isn't anything else I can do. There's six of them now and Fly at least half the year. We're going to have spread out come spring. We'll put those fallow acres on the far side to corn, besides all the fields we planted this spring. Horse is old. We need a young, strong mule. And we're going to need more livestock. We've got to build another room to sleep all them boys. They all have to have clothes. We need lots and lots of things around here, Lucy, and this is the only way I know to get any cash money. I've been studying on it for a long time. I just can't see any other way."

I stitched away at my sewing and didn't say nothing.

"I do not like it, Lucy, leaving you like this, and I don't blame you if you don't like it either. But I just can't see no other way."

I thought of the few gold pieces left in my oilskin pocket. Just a bit put by in case of emergency. Sure not make a drop in the bucket for what he said we had to do. "Isn't there any money left at all?" I asked.

"Yeah, some. Enough for a few things. But I can't leave you without a gun, so that means another one for me, plus powder and shot for both. And a poke of trail grub to tote, and a few odds and ends. And I'll leave you the rest just in case. There's enough for that, but not enough to get us started come spring."

Well, I could see he was right, but I still didn't like it. Wasn't going to neither, not never, as Jim Beam would say. But there was nothing I could do about it, and I never did set no store in a whiny woman.

"Well, Mr. Shields, if you have to, then I reckon you have to. When do you plan on leaving?"

"Pretty soon. I'll be going north and should be on my way afore snow flies."

"You've got to have traps."

"I have them. In the barn. Old ones, but good ones. I've got them all cleaned up already." I nodded. That was what he'd been doing in the barn all this time.

"I reckon I'll go to town tomorrow and get what I have to have. I'll bring you more powder and shot, Lucy. You had better keep the gun loaded and don't you be afraid to shoot it."

I nearly laughed at that. Scared to shoot? Not me! Not Lucy Shields. Shoot first and ask questions after, I would.

That was all. The man was going north into the wild country to trap out the winter. Then he'd sell the pelts to get the money to work the farm come spring.

I don't know why I was so dead set against it. It wasn't that I couldn't manage here with the young'uns. I could do right-well with the boys' help. We had food and plenty of firewood, though I could chop firewood just fine if I had to. Had the gun, did I need it. Had ol' Horse and the wagon, did I need them. I couldn't see where anything would come up as couldn't be handled.

No. Wasn't that. Think it must have been the man himself. I just couldn't take to the idea of him legging it all over the territory alone. I shook myself. There was nothing to fret about. He was a married man now. But then, he'd been married to Lizbeth when Pudge was born. Yeah, and Chunk and Short, too. Yeah, and throw Fly in for good measure for all I knew!

Of course, I wasn't poorly like Lizbeth, and it was his own darned contrariness that kept him bedded in the barn. Well, there was nothing I could do. But something he'd better do, and that was to have a right good care where he bedded those fiddle feet of his whilst he was gone! Did he fetch me another woods colt I sure wasn't going to take kindly to it! And I wasn't puny like Lizbeth either!

Next day the man went to town. It was crisp, nipping cold. Too cold for snow, but you could smell it coming. Wouldn't be long now until real winter would be on us. The man had waited as long as he could. He'd have to leave in the next couple of days.

When he came back from town, he brought the powder and shot he had promised, and he also brought a small parcel I had especially asked for.

It seemed that the parcels he had brought for himself were sure scant.

Chapter Thirteen

The next day, Flying Cloud came home, and the day after that, the man left.

Nothing showed in Fly's face, but his eyes glittered and I knew he was disappointed at not being taken along. The man couldn't take him. He had lost the weight he had gained during the late spring and early summer he had spent at the Square. He was now as thin as he had been when I first saw him. It struck me that he was taller and somehow there was more the look of the man about him. But he could not have stood the long cold winter trip his pa had planned.

The man and me didn't talk about it, we just knew. Both of us. "You'll be here, Fly, when I get back. You keep that gun loaded, Lucy."

And then he was gone.

What Fly thought of the increase in the family since he had been gone, I sure couldn't guess. He made no comment but got along well with all of them. Toady and the twins goggled at him, but Pudge took to him like a long-lost friend. If Fly squatted against the hearth wall, Pudge was sure to wedge his misshapen little self down tight next to him and, looking up into Fly's handsome red-gold face, he'd chatter his strange gibberish and boom his deep little laugh.

I didn't worry. Fly would cover his bones with meat and it wouldn't take long now that he was home. I didn't have to look twice at him to know two things. Fly was starting to grow up and the food in the lodge of Howl-of-the-Wolf was scarce. On that score, I was right, for Flying Cloud ate that night like there was no tomorrow. A strange look flew over his face when I seated him in the man's place. I patted his shoulder.

"You're the eldest, Fly. You will have to be the man of the family until your Pa gets back."

Naturally, Jim Beam couldn't let it go at that, "Hey! Fly!" he shouted, "You sure makes some Pa! Yeah! You sure does! Hey, Pa! Can I have four bits? Hey, Pa! Do I have to work tomorrow, huh, Pa? Hey, Pa! Tell Ma to make some of that there pully candy."

He bellowed with laughter and Toady was about on the point of joining him when I fixed him good.

"And if he told me to and if I made that pully candy, you wouldn't get any just for being so ornery!"

He immediately forgot Fly's new position. "Aw!" he screamed, "Ma! Ya' wouldn't! Aw, Beth! She wouldn't! Fly, you tell her! Aw, she wouldn't!"

"Then you just sit and eat, Jim Beam, and we'll see after supper."

Then, of course, I had to make the candy and, of course, I wouldn't give to any of them if I didn't give to Jim Beam.

And while we pulled and they ate, I told them another story. Pudge squealed to have Tom Thumb, but I told them about the boy who cried wolf. The little ones goggled, so fascinated they almost forgot to eat.

Fly took to the cot the man placed in a corner for him with a good will, and I'm sure he felt he was truly at home.

Two days later, the first snow fell. It was light and it didn't stick long and the young'uns enjoyed it a lot. They all ran and threw snow balls, even Beth, and Lost Be behaved like she'd lost her wits. She dashed out as if she was going to conquer the world, baying and chasing the young'uns. Then she tried to eat up all the snow around her, and when she couldn't, she tip-toed through the rest! Yes, she did! And she caught a snowball and tried to bring it into the house.

And so, we began winter living in the Square. The chores were simple, mostly just caring for the animals. The boys took care of that. On a dry day, I set them to mending and patching the harness. They cleaned out the barn and bedded the animals new. I climbed up in the loft and looked at the man's place. He had some small comforts. Looked like he'd been bedding there for some time.

Beth and I sewed. I measured out the wool that was left. Jim Beam and Toady could each have a coat. Squeezing it carefully, I could get one for Pudge, his being so little. There was yarn to knit Fly a sweater to go under his buckskin jerkin. I cut and stitched away and Beth knit under my keen eye and, presently, the four eldest boys were warmly dressed.

Pudge strutted up and down the floor with his bandy-legged, shoulder-swaggering strut.

"Zee zat!" he screeched, "Pidge preety!" And he gabbled in his jargon.

They laughed at him. He laughed with them, but it was many long years before we really gentled Pudge.

I dug from my trunk my new heavy cloak. Coats were made for Chunk and Short out of its tail, and I managed a cape and a tiny hood for Beth. She squiggled as she hadn't done in weeks.

I smiled. She could get out and she would be warm. My old cloak would do a while yet for me. I wasn't going anyplace this winter except the barn, and I reckoned Hog and Moon Eyes and Biddy and Horse didn't care about my cloak.

I brought a pile of corn shucks into the pantry and, come the first snow that lasted several days, I set them all to plaiting their own straw hats. And then soon the corn shucks were gone and the straw hats stood on a shelf in a stack.

The weather cleared, it dried, and several days later we had a light snow that stuck overnight.

The boys had gone out to the barn to care for the animals, and they dashed back in, the milk slopping from Toady's pail, their eyes as big as saucers.

"Ma! Quick, come and see!" shouted Jim Beam, "Hurry! Come and see. They're gonna get ate up! They are! Come on, Ma, hurry!"

So, I hurried. They drug me out around the barn. I stared. There were the tracks. I guess I could have followed them all the way to the woods, they were that plain. Bigger than Lost Be's, and with big gouging nails and placed with a long stride. Wolf! A wolf, after the barn animals—most likely the chicks and pheasants. Maybe Moon Eyes. Don't reckon even one this big would tangle with Hog. And I doubt with Horse, in these confined quarters.

Well, didn't matter what he was after. Everything here had come to me too hard. I didn't reckon to lose any of it. I calmed right down and I '*pish-tish*'ed the young'uns.

"Oh. It's nothing," I told them. "He'll go away when he finds out he can't get anything."

They jumped at me. Jim Beam yelled concern about Hog, Toady was anxious over Moon Eyes and Pudge screamed alarmingly about Horse.

Chunk, or was it Short, looked at me with tears in his eyes. "Don't let him get Biddy, Ma. You can't let him."

"Now, you just don't fret." I told them, "He isn't going to get a single one of our family."

And that's how come that, after the young'uns were abed and asleep that night, I measured extra loads and, making sure the gun was loaded, I slipped the powder and shot into my apron pocket. I put on my cloak and went to take my vigil in the barn.

Come another year and Lost Be could be put on to a wolf and most likely kill it. Or, leastwise, trounce it well enough to make it stay shy of the neighborhood. She was coming up to be as ugly and as vicious as her mother already.

But right now, I couldn't wait for that. I wasn't fixing to lose so much as a single pullet, nor was I going to tolerate the skulking about of a wolf. Never did know when we'd be needing game and him laying out there in the woods as big as you please and killing everything in sight. No! Nor prowling my barn! And not scaring my young'uns, neither. No. Reckon I wasn't going to hold still for that. Not at all!

So, I settled myself down as comfortable as I could be with the gun by my side to wait for the wolf. I must have waited quite a spell, reckon until near daylight, and I suspect I dozed some, because first thing I knew, Horse neighed out real loud like. The silly pullet who had nested in my lap flew straight up into my face, Moon Eyes baa-ed, Hog squealed, and I shot a hole in the barn roof!

That wasn't all I did neither. I came out that barn door shooting in every direction, pushing in the shot and powder as fast as I could.

The house door burst open, and Lost Be dashed out baying fit to kill. The young'uns followed right on her heels. My last shot went off in the air due to my yanking the gun up. I reckoned I better not shoot any more, might hit one of the young'uns or even that baying idiot dog!

I hoped Pudge hadn't landed on Beth when he tumbled out of the cubby!

I caught my breath and tried to look around. Darn that silly pullet! I'd sure wring her neck did I ever find out which one she was.

Seemed to me the young'uns all shouted at once. All except Fly. Of course, he never shouted nothing. Seemed, too, like they all shouted something different. I couldn't make out to understand none of them. Wasn't that just the way with a bunch of contrary young'uns?

I splashed the gun butt down in the puddle I was standing in and I yelled as loud as I could, "Hush!"

They hushed and I never did see such a passel of saucer sized eyes.

I got my bearings, and I looked around. It was raining dismally and every single one of those young'uns was a-standing there shivering and shaking and turning blue in their night drawers. That is, all except Beth, she was in her night shift, but it was all about the same. She was shivering and shaking and turning blue, too!

"What are all of you doing standing around out here in the rain?" I demanded. "Haven't you got any better sense than that?"

And then Jim Beam cut loose. You could have heard him a mile away. "You shot him, Ma! You did! Yeah! You did! Hey, didn't she Fly? Hey, Toady! Hey, Pudge! Beth, you tell her! She done it! Yeah, Ma! Shot that ol' wolf! Yeah! Did! Look at that, Ma! My, ain't he monstrous! Just monstrous!"

I stared around. Yeah. I'd shot him. Poor old thing. Didn't have no better sense than to come a-sniffling around Lucy Shields' critters! Didn't look hardly no more than skin and bones and his fur all muddied and slicked down with the rain. His feet looked to be twice the size of the rest of him and his head with those great big ears. And Lost Be a-worrying at him. I aimed a good swipe at her. That was one kill I wasn't at all proud of.

But to keep us all from freezing, I finally said Fly could skin him out and peg the hide on the inside of the barn door. Don't know what it is about boys that sometimes makes you think they are meaner than God ever meant them to be. Jim Beam howled to the roof top because I wouldn't let him feed that old wolf to Hog.

I couldn't never take a bite out of old Hog no matter when he was butchered, did I let him have one mouthful of that mangey wolf. Might be that was waste. I didn't care.

I let Fly take his pelt on his promise that he'd see to it that the carcass was buried. I left him and Jim Beam and Toady and Pudge standing out there.

Well, they buried the wolf, or leastwise I suppose they did, because I saw no more of him except his hide pegged out on the inside of the barn door. And when Fly had cured that hide and brushed it out well, it looked right good and full. Horse neighed his discontent but didn't do him any good.

The young'uns looked at me kinda strange-like for the rest of the day, but that old wolf's coming, and his going, got swallowed up in everyday happenings before long.

I gave the gun over into Jim Beam's hands and he climbed on a stool and hung it back on the old deer's horns. But it was loaded, and powder and shot lay on the shelf underneath it.

Jim Beam didn't mince words. He never did. He strutted in front of the hearth. "See that!" he shouted for the edification of all the young'uns. "That's ol' gun! Don't nobody touch ol' gun! You hear me? Don't nobody—nobody don't touch ol' gun except for me! Nobody! You hear me?"

Short, or was it Chunk, goggled at him, "Not even Fly, Jim Beam?" he whispered.

"Aw! Fly knows that's my ol' gun." Jim Beam bristled, "And he'll help me whomp on any of you who touches it! Ain't that right, Fly?"

It was right. Fly didn't say anything, but his black eyes glittered and he didn't even look at them.

I nodded over my sewing. Yes, Fly was teaching them the way he'd been taught. I could sleep easy. No young'un would touch that gun. No, not even our wild little Pudge.

And they didn't. And I have to tell you, Lucy Shields would think a second time before she ever took that gun down again. I couldn't shoot! I had heard my brothers talk, I knew all the right words, but *Lucy didn't need to waste shot.* She'd never have to shoot. I didn't teach Jim Beam to shoot. I simply spouted phrases I'd heard. He was a natural. He had gone on his own! Sure, I knew how to load a gun. What woman didn't? But I couldn't shoot and the hole in the barn roof proved that.

Pudge mended it. He scrabbled up that roof like he was walking the corn field. I gave him an extra pat on the head that night. Pudge and I might not speak the same language, but we didn't need to.

Jim Beam shoved his chin up and shouted his thoughts and you could make sure that he meant exactly what he said. Fly stared at me in that peculiar, flat-faced way he always had. Toady had a way of tucking his head down and flashing his eyes and stopping just short of what he meant to say. I found myself playing dumb and then snapping him up short. He rewarded me with that wide grin that really set me to thinking.

We were snow bound many a day that winter and I watched those young'uns. Oh, sure, Jim Beam was cock-o'-the-walk, no doubt about it. Yet he deferred just the least bit to Fly. Fly knew this and his eyes glittered. God save me, I didn't want to be around if it ever came to a showdown between those two.

Jim Beam's emotions were nearer the surface than Toady's, and Jim Beam struck out swiftly if he thought it necessary. He quelled Toady instantly, but only by Toady's acquiescence. Once in my life I saw them fight. It was only thanks to Toady's good sense that they were both still alive at the end of that fight.

Jim Beam, once started, couldn't stop. He would kill or he would die on the spot. Jim Beam was one way and there was never any doubt about that.

Pudge—well one could never say that Pudge was much besides just Pudge. He loved all things alive, and he believed that they should not be hated for what nature had made them. He would stand with every ounce of his tiny strength for the right of a frog to hop. He deplored the pouring of boiling water down an ant hill. He never stepped on a spider. He braved a screech owl over a wounded mouse. He defended all life, and he hesitated not to challenge Jim Beam. He would fling himself out and catch Jim Beam furiously. "Jeem!" he would shriek and follow it with a lot of gibberish.

Jim Beam would catch his little fist and shout, "That's my brother! If you don't like it, I'll punch your nose!" And so, Pudge always won his point. Jim Beam would have stood against even Flying Cloud for Pudge.

This had nothing to do with the relationship between Beth and Jim Beam. Beth was feeling the pressure of being the only female in a bunch of males, and I have to say she held it well. She bowed to Fly as eldest brother, and yet she always conveyed, somehow or another, that this was with Jim Beam's permission. Always this brother came first in her thoughts, and she made few bones about it. At least so far as Jim Beam was concerned, she didn't. She picked at Toady a little, stood firmly beside Pudge, and mothered the two little ones fondly. As tiny as Beth was, there was plenty of her to go around.

I looked at Chunk and Short. They were young yet, but their natures were beginning to gel. Easy they were, and could be managed to a point. After that, they reared back, bowed their legs, set their feet, and they couldn't be budged.

I looked at them all with understanding. All this I saw, but there were changes yet to come. They weren't grown up yet! I was still physically supreme and right now I held the reins. After me would come the man. When his authority was worn out, so be it. Meantime, just set loose, Lucy, bide your time.

Chapter Fourteen

It was snowing light and feathery on top of a lying snow when we went out for the tree. I didn't want to go too far from the Square even though Jim Beam stepped light and carried the gun. And so, it happened that the tree had one scant side instead of being full around. That didn't matter.

We sat it next to the door against the wall.

Of course, it sat down pretty low to the floor because Jim Beam and Toady took turns sawing off the trunk to get it even on the bottom. They didn't get it even until they got nearly to the lower branches, but we didn't care about that either. Matter-of-fact, they were all quite pleased about it and I reckoned it was just as well. There was a piddling little next to nothing to go under it, so the closer the branches, the smaller the space to fill.

I took my shears, and I snipped out small pieces of light material, scraps that I'd saved, and I showed the young'uns to dip them in sugar water and press them down over the bottom of a tin cup. Then I pulled and twisted the raggedy edges so that, when it was dry, it formed a pretty shaped shell. They watched almost without words while I stitched into the bottom of it, snipped my thread, and tied it on a branch.

They "oohed" and "awed" and set about finding all manner of objects to press the scraps over to make different shapes. I held onto my shears and snipped the scraps for them. Pudge's hands were too little to work the heavy handles and I sure didn't want Chunk or Short brandishing their long points about.

I fashioned a bright red star out of a wisp of ribbon and Fly tied it to the very top. I'm afraid that Beth didn't get to make very many herself, for the boys kept her busy stitching into the backs of theirs and passing them to Fly to tie on.

I took some of the finest of the dried corn and put it in the skillet and shook it back and forth on the spider. The first kernel that popped sent Jim Beam scrabbling for the gun.

"What's that?" he yelled.

I tipped the lid just the littlest bit and a kernel popped and flew out. Lost Be pounced on it and swallowed it before he could hardly see it.

"That's a little corn I'm popping," I told him, "I reckon that you can see how good it is since Lost Be gobbled it down so quick and it still being so hot!"

"Can we eat it?" he shouted.

"Can And we're gonna string some too and hang it on the Christmas tree."

"Hang it on the what?" Toady demanded, staring at me.

And while I popped a good, great big bowl of corn, Beth told the story of Christmas. Every now and again Jim Beam would holler, "Aw! Ain't so!" and Beth would look at me. I'd nod and she'd say, "Yes, it is, Jim Beam," and go on with her story.

I looked at them all sitting around the table working together and laughing and talking, excited and happy, with the elder ones helping the younger ones. I wished I could keep them that way forever. But then they had to grow up and life wasn't always that easy. Poor tykes. Every one of them had cause to know life was plenty hard at times. I wished the man was there to see them.

When they finished their decorations, I put the popped corn on the table and hunted needles and thread for them. They ate and they strung, but mostly they ate, and the white strings we eventually hung on the tree were short. We had to string them well up in the branches because Chunk—or was it Short?—hung his low and Lost Be ate it, thread and all.

Pudge nibbled his until there was hardly anything left except the tiny, hard, yellow kernels, but he insisted it be hung anyway, and he thought it was beautiful. I never did see any boy that could eat as much as Pudge.

I reckoned I'd done right by waiting until Christmas Eve before starting all this. None of them had ever had a Christmas before, leastwise not one they remembered, and it was right hard for them to wait even this one night. Seemed to me they weren't going to bed down quiet until dawn.

But finally, they did, and I took my small bundle and knelt down in front of that tree. I looked up at it and I knew it was a Christmas tree I would never forget. I had seen bigger and finer trees in my brothers' houses, but I had never seen one so beautiful as this one. Sure, the branches were too close to the floor. Sure, it sat a little aslant. Its decorations faced up or down or out, depending on how they'd been tied. Short's (Or was it Chunk's?) popcorn string was awful short because he'd eaten most of it. Pudge's was nibbled, but it held the place of honor just below my star. Fly had hoisted Pudge atop his shoulders to string it with his own tiny hands.

No. There would never be another tree like this. There, on the middle branches, lay Beth's string. Longest of all, because she had eaten the least. True, it was dragged down on one end because Lost Be liked popcorn and, taking her chances, had snatched at it. How like them that Toady's string lay full and white, deep within the green boughs, and Jim Beam's strung bold and tight on the tips of the branches. How strangely like Fly that his curled among the scant branches to the back. Odd how much you could tell about people, even young ones, if you just knew where to look.

I opened my bundle, and I had to slap Lost Be's nose out of it. I didn't for a minute think to wish for more. I was glad just to have what I had. I laid them out on the white towel under the tree. All except Beth's. Hers I propped high in the tree, against its sturdy trunk.

I sat back and I looked a long time before I made sure Lost Be was asleep on the hearth and blew out the candle. I slept the minute I hit the bed.

That was a good thing, too, because it was Jim Beam's eagle eye that spotted the presents next morning and he whooped from the cubby. Half-awake, I had sense enough to screech out, "Pudge! No, no! Pudge, No!"

So he followed Jim Beam down the ladder. They didn't dash in upon the tree but hung back peering and "oohing" and "awing" and whispering among themselves.

I knelt down and I handed out the presents. I handed them out according to age and I handed them out slow to prolong their happy excitement.

The first present was for Fly, and it was not new. That is, it hadn't just been bought. It was a Christmas present I had received myself some years ago from Buck. Secretly, I had always suspected I had gotten it because Becky wouldn't wear it and neither would I, but it was perfect for Fly. It was a long gold chain, nearly the size of my finger, and its pendant was an elongated blue stone worked about with gold filigree.

The young ones gasped, and Fly's eyes gleamed surprisingly, so I hurried on.

Jim Beam was next, and his present was a hunting knife and sheath. For once, I saw Jim Beam stand silent.

Toady was next, and his was a pocketknife with three blades. He fell back silent, too.

Pudge was next, and I pulled him against my knee while I waited for him to unwrap it. He stared at it and there was such confusion, such vulnerability on his face that I took it quickly to my own mouth. I could tongue a mouth harp right well and I sure did then. He fell back from me sitting down flat on his little bottom and staring with great eyes. I played a short little ditty. That was just as well, because he leaped up, snatched it from me, and, dancing about the room, he blew great blasts of noise.

We clapped our hands and laughed, and Jim Beam sprang after him, "Hey, Pudge!" he yelled, "You play and I'll jig."

And they did. Pudge drew great breaths and blew them tunelessly through the harp and did Jim Beam dance! Of course, it wasn't like any jig I ever did see before. I reckon it was more of a knife dance, you might say. Because Jim Beam pulled his knife from its sheath and danced, sheath in one hand and knife in the other. Well, whatever it was, it was beautifully savage, but I had to put a stop to it. Looked to me like Jim Beam might slice off Pudge's head in his excitement.

But Jim Beam didn't sheath his knife nor Pudge stop his blowing.

I gave to the twins next, half a dozen tiny lead soldiers each. That was all, as far as they were concerned. Right then they set up a battle, and it took them days to argue out who was winning.

Deliberately, I left Beth's until last. I reached down the doll, and I put it into her hands.

This was really from me and from Toady, because I had used the time he gave me by milking Moon Eyes to make this doll, and it was the prettiest one I could possibly make. It had an embroidered face and braided yarn hair, and its clothes came off and on.

Beth cried. She snatched that little doll to her face and she cried all over its pretty clothes.

I kissed her little bent head and went to cook breakfast.

I thought Christmas was a great success. And so, it was. It took the boys all of half an hour to start arguing.

Jim Beam leaped into the middle of the floor shouting, "Shut that, Pudge! You just shut! How am I gonna tell you what I'm gonna do with my knife with you caterwauling like that?"

Pudge wasn't about to shut. He flung himself at Jim Beam, "Jeem!" he screeched, "Pidge blow! Pidge blow!"

I held my knife up. I wondered if it was about time for Jim Beam's bottom to be tanned again?

No. Not yet. Fly slid in quick-like. Somehow his fingers looked so brown and strong against Pudge's little fists. He lifted the mouth harp up. "Blow, my little brother, blow," he almost crooned.

"That's what I said!" screeched Jim Beam, "He can blow when I ain't talking. I ain't talking now! Blow, Pudge, blow!"

And believe you me, Pudge blew! I let him, too. Served Jim Beam right. But after a while I caught him up and set him on the sideboard.

I hummed at him. He put the harp down. I tapped the right square with my knife tip. He blew. It was a jumble of sound. He put the harp down and looked to me again in question. I tapped again with my knife and showed him the tip of my tongue. He was so quick. He caught on right then. Before the day was out, I had him blowing a tune.

I was awfully pleased. None of the other gifts had fretted me as Pudge's had. But I had guessed right. He gave us some bad days while he learned, but after that, he keened out the most heart-rending sounds ever. But Pudge's music was inside of Pudge, and he kept it mostly that way.

Beth favored Jim Beam and named her doll "Tildy." Tildy got up with us in the morning and went to bed with us at night. She had her clothes taken off a thousand times a day. And then, for the sake of propriety, she had them put on equally as many times.

Jim Beam's knife went on his belt whenever he went out, and Toady got into the habit of slapping his pockets to be sure of his knife. Fly strung his present about his neck and kept it there. Chunk and Short sprawled full length, belly-down on the floor to be stepped over until I nearly got out of patience with their battles.

But then the weather got really bad. We strung a rope from the barn door to the house. The first couple of times I fought my way out with the boys. After that, I let them go alone. They got along right well the first few times, but then, right in the middle of a blizzard and the snow pelting down so hard and swirling so in the wind that you couldn't see your hand in front of your face, the rope, wet and stretched, slid off its peg on the door and Jim Beam, clinging to the end of it, was lost somewhere between the barn and the house. I hoped he had sense enough to hang onto the end of the rope. He did.

We couldn't see him, but we could sure hear him! I held to the door and took Toady by the hand with Fly grasping onto the other end of Toady.

I took my first chance when he stopped for a breath and I hollered as loud as I could, "You're off to one side, Jim Beam. Keep that rope taut and walk this way. We'll catch you as you go by."

Jim Beam told us at the top of his lungs that it was a "durned ol' barn," a "durned ol' rope," "durned ol' snow," and a few other "durned ol'" things, but he must have heard me because it sounded like he was coming nearer.

I shook my head. Didn't reckon we could lose anything that made that much noise. And sure enough, we didn't. We did miss him the first two times he went by, and I never did see how he could have managed that. But then, there was no accounting for most things Jim Beam did. The third time he was floundering along as fast as he could go in the deep snow and shouting, and he slammed smack dab into Toady.

They went down in a heap and Toady's tightening hand drug Fly into them. Jim Beam came up still yelling. "Hey! Hey, ya' fellers! Hey! How come you got me losted? How come? Hey!"

"Let go of the rope, Jim Beam!" Toady shouted back, "Let go!"

"Can't!" hollered Jim Beam, "I tied it on! Sure, I did!"

I shooed Toady and Fly into the house, and it took me a while to get Jim Beam untied. He'd tied near a dozen knots, and he'd tied them tight. The rope bit into his arm.

"Confound it, Jim Beam!" my teeth were chattering from the cold, "If I ever get you loose from this here rope, I'm gonna teach you to tie a proper knot! What made you do a thing like that?"

"I didn't want to get losted off that ol' rope! Sure didn't! No, Siree! Didn't! What's the matter with my knots? They're dandy knots. They're good and tight, ain't they? Tied 'em, I did! They're just dandy!"

I had to call back into the house and borrow Fly's knife. I cut the rope.

"For sure! They're just dandy knots, Jim Beam! And you can just get in there by the fire and untie them yourself. Let's see if you like untying as well as you did tying them!"

I pieced out the shortened rope with a dish towel and fastened it back to its peg. Time to do something more about it in the morning when, maybe, we could see. Sure didn't want to lose that loose end though. Might be the only way we had of getting to the animals in the barn for who knew how long.

Well, it took Jim Beam some time to get that rope's end off his arm. All the young'uns took a turn, but it was finally Pudge's strong little fingers that worked those awful twisty knots loose. Jim Beam's arm was striped angry red and dead white, but the skin wasn't broken. Beth rubbed it and made a fuss over him, but I just let him learn. Bet he'd never tie himself to anything in that fashion again!

He played that arm up as much as he could. He winced and held to it and moaned whenever he thought of it for two days. And he shouted the story of when he was "losted on the end of ol' rope" 'til I could have shook him good. And just when I was on the verge, he gave me a better way. He asked me for a sling to carry his injured arm.

"Well," I drawled at him, "sure, Jim Beam, I will. When you're bleeding all over and the bones are sticking out of your skin."

Fly's gleaming eyes slewed away, and Toady's head dipped to hide his smile. The rest of them goggled at me, and Jim Beam, he had the biggest stare of all. His mouth gaped open and his eyes bugged out. But his arm got well right quick, and I never heard him tell that story again.

Chapter Fifteen

It was the middle of January, and we got a little relief from the snow. It turned out to be too cold to snow and what lay on the ground was coated with a thin layer of ice. The air was clear and so sharp it stung. Of course, we'd get more snow, more blizzards in February and the weather would not get comfortable at least until March.

The Croaker was coming up to his full growth and Biddy would start laying soon and the pullets not too long after. Moon Eyes would kid in April and be freshened for spring and summer.

I went out to the smoke house and replenished the pantry. I killed and hung three of the pheasant hens. Chunk and Short hung on my heels so afraid were they for Biddy. I tried to explain that Biddy was my setting hen and I wasn't about to wring her neck. But they followed me anyhow.

They watched me kill the pheasants, and two hours later, both of them and Biddy were gone.

I took Jim Beam and Fly and we followed their tracks in the snow. They were clear and it was obvious that they carried an object, probably poor Biddy between them. There were the flat kind of oblong marks between their footprints where they'd humped something down every few steps.

I was beginning to really get worried when we finally came on them. They were sitting flat in the snow, their feet stuck straight out before them, and on their laps lay a thumping and clucking gunny sack. The tears were frozen on their cheeks. It gave me a jerk, it did, the look of them.

They looked so lost, so forlorn, so kind of at bay.

One of them screamed at me, "No! You ain't gonna kill Biddy! You ain't!"

"We're gonna go get Pa!" screeched the other, "He won't let you!"

That gave me another turn. Poor little tykes. Hardly found a Pa and he was gone. I hardened my heart. I couldn't have them running off every time they took a notion. Next time might not be so easy to find them.

I stepped forward and yanked that gunny sack right out of their hands. Then I stuck my arm down in it and pulled Biddy out by the legs. I let her hang down at my side.

I took a deep breath because I didn't like what I had to do. But I cured them of running away right then.

"Git!" I said as sternly as I could, "You get back to that house! And if you stop or you turn around, I'm gonna whack you a good one with this here hen! Now git!"

They got. One of them fell down and the other pulled him up and they kept going. I think I would have risked Biddy's life to thwack Jim Beam had he opened his mouth. He did not. He and Fly followed me while I drove the little ones home.

They cried. I let them. Better they should cry now, when they were safe than that someday they should sit in the woods and cry and freeze to death when I couldn't find them. I drove them right to the door.

"Get in there!" I ordered.

I turned Biddy over to Fly and Jim Beam to be put back on her nest. The twins were chilled through.

"Get to bed!" I snapped.

Beth startled.

Again, they got. Wasn't any time at all until they were sound asleep.

I put off my cloak and sat down tiredly at the table. "Toady, you go to the barn and help the boys. You too, Pudge."

They went without a word. Beth's great eyes fastened on my face.

"They're alright, ain't they, Ma?" she murmured.

"Yes," I nodded.

She dared a little grin, "I don't reckon they'll do that again, Ma."

"Nope, I don't reckon," I answered.

And just like I said, Beth seemed to know hidden things, because she hustled round and she dipped her little hands into my precious tiny tin of tea and she set out the cups. The boys came in, quiet for once.

"Why don't you just set a spell, Ma?" she asked, "Maybe Pudge'll play for you."

And Pudge played. He wedged himself down next to Fly against the hearth wall and he gulped his sweet hot tea. Then he played. Soft, wild, sweet tunes. Fly cupped his tin mug of tea in his hands and its steam drifted up in front of his half-closed eyes.

Jim Beam and Toady sat with Beth and me at the table. Presently, I began to simmer down and things began to get real again.

I started supper and Beth got up the twins and gave them some hot, sweet tea. I nodded at her. I didn't want them to miss supper. They were skinny enough.

But at suppertime, I made myself plain. "Fly, tomorrow morning I want you to get out and find me a nice birch tree. And when you find that tree, fetch me a piece, oh, about this big," I showed him my finger, "and about this long," I measured about a yard between my hands. "And I want it to be nice and whippy like. When you find it and bring it back, why reckon I want it put up there on Jim Beam's deer horns."

Jim Beam fell into my trap. "Why, Ma? What do you want that for?" he demanded loudly.

"Why?" I looked at him real flat-like, "I can't always run out and catch a chicken if I need to whup a boy. I reckon I'll just have a handy birch rod up there beside the gun and then I can always reach it, do I need to whup some boy."

Next day Fly fetched in a birch rod and laid it alongside of the gun. Oddly enough, that rod was never lifted down again. And more to the point, Chunk and Short never ran away again.

My next problem was one that could not be handled by the birch rod, nor any other kind I ever heard of.

The boys were in the barn where I let them play at times, it being bigger than the house.

Beth sidled up near me.

"Ma?" she paused so long I stopped my work to look at her, "Ma, Toady's not my brother, is he?"

It shocked me a little, but I went on with my sewing, "Well, no, I reckon not." I shook my head.

"I'm glad he isn't," she stated solemnly.

I jerked, but I didn't say nothing. She spoke again and I shoved my needle into my finger, put the finger into my mouth and stared at her.

"I reckon I'm gonna marry Toady, Ma."

"Well," I tried to be calm, "I have to tell you, Beth, I think that maybe you're a mite too young to decide something like that just yet."

She pulled her eyes back and stitched away for a minute. Then she flat-faced me, "No, I don't think so, Ma," she answered. "I'm just guessing that I can't marry no man but Toady."

I swallowed. "Now, Beth, Toady isn't a grown man yet. You're going to meet a lot of boys and a lot of men before you're old enough to marry. You'd best not to be setting your mind so soon, honey."

She dropped her eyes back to her sewing. "I reckon its done set, Ma," she murmured.

Well, guess that wasn't the only time that winter that I wished her Pa was back because I really needed him, but it was right up there.

I watched them, those two children. Beth snapped at Toady and even hit him. Toady grinned and tucked his head. Well, I suspected that romance would keep. Not only until the man was back, but most likely for some years. Take Toady five years to hit sixteen and Beth a year behind him. Plenty of time to start worrying then if she didn't change her mind in the meantime.

And then it was February, and we were buffeted again and again by blizzards. It got so there was only snow and nothing but snow. It was hard to believe that this great white expanse had ever been anything else but white mush.

With the beginning of March, the sun came out. It had little warmth, and the snow and ice melted slowly. There were small snow flurries that laid light coverings over the ice crust.

Moon Eyes kidded. One night she was alone, then the next morning, she had twin kids with her. Toady took his blanket and slept with them for two nights. Then they coated out enough to keep warm, and we were proud owners of a young nanny and a billy. I couldn't have been more pleased. We were well on our way to our own goat herd.

Chunk and Short came down with serious head colds, and how Toady missed catching it, him sleeping with them, I'll never know. But he did. I kept them in the trundle, but don't reckon they were very sick. Half the time they fought and half the time they set up battles with their soldiers in the tent they made out of their blankets using their round heads for tent poles. After two days, I gave up and let them get out of bed. Didn't seem to make much difference to them. They still split the day between fighting and playing. After I got tired of walking over them, they began to set up their soldiers on my big bed. But when I'd slept one night on two of those sharp little lead fellows, I put a stop to that. I made them take them off to the trundle and if Toady did not like sleeping on those bits of lead, he could just throw them out on the floor. But Toady was Toady, and he didn't seem to know whether he slept on the toy soldiers or not. He woke up every morning with a grin.

And then one day, just when I'd finished some make-do washing and strung it in the pantry to dry, Jim Beam gave me a good turn.

CHAPTER SIXTEEN

I could hear him yelling long before he ever got to the house.

"What's he saying?" I demanded of Beth, but she just stared at me with those great big violet eyes.

I jerked open the door. Jim Beam was running as fast as his legs would go and Lost Be leaping all around him and baying fit to kill. I couldn't make heads nor tails out of what he was screeching until he got to me.

"Hey, Ma!" he bellowed loud enough to split an ear drum. "Get out, Lost Be! Hey, Ma! Pa's here! Yeah! He is! He came back. He did! Hey, Ma!"

I just stood there, kind of dumb-like, wiping my hands on my apron.

"Hey, Ma!" shouted Jim Beam, "Ma, didn't you hear me? Hey, Beth! Pa's back! He is! Yeah! And he brought company!"

Company! I slicked back my hair. "Beth, you change your apron! Jim Beam! Shut that squawking! Fetch a pail of water!"

It was a little early, but I started dinner anyhow. Reckoned the man would be good and hungry and plenty tired of his own cooking. And company! The first since the Colbeys. I couldn't help but wonder who it was.

Jim Beam sloshed down the full water bucket on the sideboard and took to his heels, making for the barn, before I could say anything more to him.

Beth and I hustled. We hustled, readied up, and I put the meal to cooking while she set the table.

The door opened and I turned away from the sideboard. He looked thinner, older. He had a new dark wool shirt. He would have to have new boots again before next winter. He stared at me.

"You're back sooner than I expected, Mr. Shields."

The man jumped when I spoke and then just stared at me like he thought I couldn't talk. That was sure a far-fetched reaction, me being Lucy. I wondered if my face was dirty or something the way he just kept looking. Well, let him. Wasn't as though he hadn't watched me plenty before.

I turned my eyes on the company.

His friend wasn't any taller than I was, but I didn't doubt that I could have lifted half again as much weight as he could from the way he was so thin and stringy. His narrow face was lined deeply and his hair, what I could see of it, was grizzled gray. He wore a fur cap and buckskins like Fly's, though his were sure a lot greasier and dirtier than any I'd ever seen on Fly. He had a hunting knife on his belt and a powder horn hanging from his shoulder. He carried his gun over his arm.

He stared at me, too. Like neither one of them could figure me out.

I looked at my husband, waiting for an introduction, but didn't seem he could do nothing but gawk. So I introduced myself. "I'm Mrs. Shields," I told the stranger. "Any friend of my husband's is welcome."

His Adams apple bobbed as he swallowed, "Thankee, ma'am," he got out. "Skinks is my name. Dan'l Skinks."

My husband stared at me worse than ever, and Beth, hanging shyly against my skirt, spoke to him, "Hello, Pa."

He drew his brows down and stared at her, "Beth?"

"Yeah, it's me, Pa."

He frowned at her and cast quick eyes around the room. It was just plain too much staring for me. I couldn't figure out what he was looking for anyhow.

"Sit down, Mr. Shields," I commanded, trying to get past all this. "We'll have an early dinner right away. Sit, Mr. Skinks . . . if you please. Beth!" I turned back to the sideboard, and I set Beth's hands to a task.

It all flew over me for just a minute. Guess, maybe he was tired, but he could have said some little word to her, *his daughter*. Couldn't see that that would have been much out of his way. And our company! Mr. Skinks was well into his middle years and didn't seem the kind of a man my husband would take for a friend.

As I cogitated on this, Beth and I got dinner done, while the man and Skinks went outside to talk. I couldn't hear what they were saying, but the man was talking fast. Skinks interrupted him a lot, but when he did, the man just kept talking faster. Neither one of them looked happy.

When a meal was finally ready on the table, I told Beth, "Run outdoors with a pan and spoon and bang up the boys." I caught up my apron tail and poured steaming hot cups of coffee for the two men. "And tell your Pa and his friend it's time to eat, too." I was a little sorry I'd used the pure coffee I'd been saving. Chicory would have been good enough, given him behaving to Beth the way he did.

The boys came in just like they always did. The twins dashed onto their stools in caps and coats, and Beth had to peel them off. They looked so big-eyed and innocent, no one would ever believe what imps they could be.

Pudge, whose talk had improved a lot since Fly had come home, rushed in, climbed up on his stool, stood atop it, as he always did, and then shed his coat and cap. He dropped them beside his stool on the floor and screamed at me, "Pidge ride horse too-day!" He boomed out his little laugh, "Geet ready! Plow! Pull wagon! Too-day ice iz gone. Pidge ride horse too-day."

I smiled and nodded at him. The man took his own regular place at the table, and I moved Skinks to Toady's stool. Jim Beam and Fly hung back as the others took their accustomed places to wait and see where they would fit. Once again, there were not enough stools or pans, and so Beth and I would wait.

"Hey, Pa!" began Jim Beam in his eternal shout, "Ya' just won't believe it, Pa, when I tell ya'! Ya' just won't! I'm gonna tell you every single thing what's happened since ya' left, Pa! It's a whoppin' lot! Hey, Fly! Hey, ain't it! A whoppin' lot, Pa!"

I almost had to laugh. It put me so in mind of my first days at the Square.

"Fly, you sit here in my place. Toady, you come here and take Beth's stool," I ordered.

Flying Cloud flashed his eyes at me, but he slid silently down on my stool. Toady balked.

"Can't take Beth's place," he mumbled stubbornly.

"Can!" I snapped at him, "You're coming up to be a man, Toady, and you eat with the men. We women-folk will eat after."

Beth's flat little chest rose. She was proud of being a part of "we women-folk." She wasn't proud enough though not to whack Toady on the shoulder with her tiny fist.

"Toady Wooten!" she hissed, "We've got company!"

Toady subsided and took the stool. Chunk (or was it Short?) reached across in front of him and fetched his twin a sound crack to the head. It knocked him off his stool. He bounced up ready to do battle.

"He was eatin' on my side of the plate!" shouted the twin, still seated.

I looked at them both flatly. "You either sit still and eat," I told them calmly, "or you go outside and fight while we eat."

That was all it took. I don't know who ate on whose side of the plate, but neither of them said another word. At the same time, Jim Beam squeezed in next to Fly and continued his shouted account of what had happened. Pudge sprung every now and then to the top of his stool to shriek a remark and boom his husky little laugh. Toady dipped his head, grinned, and slid his words in with the impact of a blow.

They laughed, they joshed each other, they squabbled familiarly, happily, just as they always did. It was loud, chaotic, but it was the sound of a happy family. Surely, it must've seemed to the man that he had never left. It seemed that way to me.

But in the midst of all that happy, healthy noise, the man slammed his cup against his plate and roared at the top of his voice to Jim Beam, "Shut that noise! *You, Boy!*"

I jerked. *You, Boy?* To Jim Beam? His own son? The man's mouth and his eyes were as wide as he could get them, like he couldn't come up with who he was talking to.

The room was deathly silent. "Jim Beam," I quietly reminded the man.

"Yeah! Er . . . ," he gulped, "Jim Beam," the man grumbled, frowning.

The uneasiness in the air was too much for Pudge. He suddenly leaped upon his stool, which startled everyone, especially the man. Pudge had barely opened his mouth to speak, when his father clipped out at him coldly, "Sit, ya' devil's imp!" And then, then without missing a beat, he turned to Fly and bellowed, "And you, ya redskin papoose, pass the milk!"

My mouth gaped open. I immediately glanced at Fly, who looked pained, but still had enough self-respect not to look away. His gaze burned into his father in a way I had never seen before. I looked back at the man with a disgust that was new to me. I had never heard such disrespect come out of his mouth, not to his kids or anyone. Something was awful wrong here. Awful wrong. Was it Skinks? Well, Mr. Skinks didn't plant my fields, nor dig my potatoes, nor milk my goat! I wasn't about to let anyone wrong my children!

"I'll ask you to remember, Mr. Shields," I said slowly through clinched teeth, "that Pudge doesn't speak too much American!" I was sharp as could be—and that was considerable—without raising my voice. "And Flying Cloud, *your eldest*, is no redder than you made him!"

I suddenly realized that I'd never talked back like that to the man before. I edged backwards towards the fireplace. Should he spring up and lift a hand to me, I'd lay him flat with the hot skillet. And Skinks right after him if need be.

The man scowled at me. "Then don't let 'em bother me!" he growled, "Can't you manage your own young'uns?"

"I can manage them right fine, considering they aren't mine!" I told him tartly. "You well know we haven't been wedded even a year yet! They're yours! All of them! Yours and Lisbeth's! Yours and an Indian girl! Yours and Marie Faberge's! Yours and Millie Wooten's! But I'm their Ma now and they are all good young'uns. And I don't intend to stand here flat-footed and let you run them down! Do you hear me, Mr. Shields?"

I backed up to the point that I could feel the heat of the fire behind me. The man inched closer to me, scowling. The skillet was at hand, and I would use it if I had to.

But turns out I didn't need it. The man stared me in the eye for a second, then burst into a loud rough roar of laughter. He slapped the table with a huge hand so sharply that all the young'uns flinched. "Hey, Skinks!" he bellowed, "Ya' see that! Full of vinegar ain't she? And pretty, too! Pretty like . . . like a lily, so pale!" He leered at me in a way that made right uncomfortable. "But with a burn like moonshine!"

I stared in disbelief. *Should I be scared?* I wondered. But as I studied the man, my fear gave way to awareness. Because, all of a sudden, there for all the world, except for size and age, was Jim Beam. It was the first time I had seen such a definite likeness, and that familiarity calmed me a bit. I swallowed hard and waited to see what would happen next.

Skinks snickered in a false sort of way, "Ya' didn't tell me ya' had a missus like her, Roan!"

"I don't tell ya' everything, Skinks!" The two men laughed, like they were in on some joke.

Good lord, Gramma Hildebrand had been right. Who could tell what I would find once I married myself off to a stranger? I had no reason to change anything I had ever thought about any of the young'uns. And yet, the man! He showed me two sides. I couldn't discount all the months that had gone before. Those months when, despite his promiscuity, he had displayed all the qualities of a good father. Those months when he had worked so hard to provide for us during the time he would be gone. Surely something had gone badly wrong. I just knew it had to be something to do with Skinks. I was sure it did.

I turned my attention to the young'uns. I put my hand across Pudge's curls in the way which had always brought me a smile. But tonight, it brought a flinch and an involuntary raising of his wee arms. It was so like the movement of that first night when he had protected his head that it brought me an awful twinge.

Deliberately, I tried to soothe Pudge. And then I laid a hand against Fly's shoulder, "Fly, you go help Pudge with ol' Horse."

Fly's black eyes gleamed. "As you say, my mother. But my brother needs little help with the horse."

I smiled at Fly and then hugged Pudge. Why was the man doing this? Why had he worked as hard, farmed out his young'uns, denied those he had to keep to get me? Why had I ever chosen Roan Shields? He was well aware of the circumstances under which we had gotten Pudge. Why did he do this now?

I didn't know the answers to these questions. I only knew that he had fooled me completely during the early months I was here. Or he'd met with some mishap during his trapping that scrambled his mind. Or else, and this was more likely, it had something to do with Skinks. For sure, the man knew me better than he pretended when Skinks was around.

While Beth cleaned up after the meal, I went with Pudge and Fly to the barn. But I was a bit shook when the man and

Skinks followed. On the way, I grabbed a pitchfork casually in hand, and shoved around a bit of the animals' bedding, just so I made it look like the pitchfork had something to do, other than what I had in mind.

Pudge was excited, as he always was around Horse. Which is exactly what I had hoped, given the way the man had treated him. I think Pudge considered Horse as his. And perhaps, in his strange existence, Horse was the only thing of which he was really sure.

Fly was with him because I had asked it, but he stopped and waited outside the stall, letting Pudge have Horse all to himself. Fly was wise in many ways.

Pudge scurried into the stall, caught up the bridle from the floor and scrambled up onto the manger. Then he started with that strange wild jargon that we were all so familiar with. Horse snorted, shied, then thrust out his nose. Pudge talked to him, petted him, and finally got the bit into his mouth and the bridle on. He flung one rein over Horse' neck. Then Pudge scurried from the manger down to the floor.

I got to grant that it looked funny. Pudge standing there, not nearly so high as Horse's leg, with one rein in his tiny hand. He shouted his jargon at the horse.

The man slapped his hand hard against the rail of the stall and bellowed his laughter. As he stepped forward, my pitchfork quivered, standing upright in the ground at his feet.

Horse bolted backwards, reared, and jerked Pudge clear off his feet. Pudge shouted more of his gibberish, and suddenly, it was repeated from beside me. It was Skinks! His roar was deep, commanding, and in the same gibberish Pudge spouted. I was right surprised! How is it that Skinks knew how to talk like Pudge?

They both shouted some more in the same crazy jargon. When Horse finally quieted, Pudge swarmed up his front leg and lay against his neck. Right on cue, Fly swung open the stall door and Horse trotted out. I stood in the darkened barn and watched Horse carry Pudge out of the stall, and then out of the barn. Finally, I relaxed against the post.

"Don't reckon yer a-gonna need that, Mrs. Shields," Skinks pulled my hand up to reveal me holding a great rusty hook I used for handling baled hay. I dropped it in disgust and walked away.

The rest of that afternoon, I kept myself to the house while the men stayed outside. I baked pies. Raisin pies. I didn't know what went on in the barn or the fields. I didn't want to know. I cooked a huge supper, even though we'd had an early, but ample, dinner when the two men first arrived. I did not know what to say to the man. Surely, he knew what I had been prepared to do with that hay-baling hook.

Beth stayed with me like my skin, but she said not a word. Lost Be was back and forth, but she walked wary of the two men, and once at a distance, bayed madly at them.

"What's wrong with yer crazy dog?" demanded the man when he came in for supper.

I shook my head, "I don't know." He knew as well as me that Lost Be didn't like strangers.

I looked at Skinks.

The boys filed in and took stools without words. Even Jim Beam was silent, though he looked as though he might burst out at any moment. Toady dipped his head and took Beth's stool without words.

The man latched on to him. "You're Toady Wooten?" he demanded.

"Yes, sir," Toady's voice was low.

"A Wooten. How'd we come by him?" he demanded of me.

"Why, as I recall, you were asked," I answered. "You said *'yes'* and here he is." Surely, there was no mystery about that.

Skinks spoke, again using the same language as Pudge. I stared. No one understood him. But upon hearing Skinks' words, our wild little Pudge's face lit up, and he was voluble. He didn't jump up on his stool. He had no need. He talked and someone answered in kind. I put my hand against his curls and was rewarded with his beautiful smile.

"How is it that you can understand Pudge's gibberish?" I asked Skinks.

"It ain't gibberish, Mrs. Shields," Skinks replied. "It's French."

I'd heard of other languages, from other countries, but never met anybody who spoke anything but the same American language we all spoke. "And how is it that you know French, Mr. Skinks?"

An evil grin spread across Skinks' face, "Tain't nobody's business but my own, Mrs. Shields," he said quietly.

The man snorted a laugh, like he and Skinks both knew something I didn't.

I did not like this Mr. Skinks *at all*. No, I did not. "Excuse me," I said to the two men. "I need to get these young'uns to bed."

The man and Skinks sat at the table until everyone was all down for the night. After I returned to the table, the man asked, "And where do we sleep?" He leered at me in a way that made my skin crawl.

I offered an extra blanket. "Here. You can share your bed in the barn," I replied.

"In the barn?" the man gasped, indignant.

I could tell he had other ideas swirling around in his head, so I had to think fast. "Well," I told him drily, "You can see I'm a bit taken up with young'uns in here. Now if you build me that room you talked about for the boys to sleep in . . . ." I let my words trail off.

He sure couldn't misunderstand that. He laughed until I thought he'd wake the young'uns, but Skinks looked solemn. Skinks took the blanket and headed out to the barn, leaving me and the man alone. He intently stared at me like a wolf stalking a chicken.

"I really have to go to bed," I snapped sharply, "Go on, get out to the barn."

The man got up and stretched himself. I didn't look. I was well aware of the look of him, and I wasn't about to fall under the power of his charms. Not now.

He grinned. "Reckon I'm gonna build that room for sleeping the boys," his voice was good natured, soft, and yet, a bit *naughty*.

"Reckon?" I snorted. "Yeah, I reckon you will."

The man looked around at all the young'uns scattered everywhere, then back at me, "If that's what it takes." He winked at me and followed Skinks out to the barn.

"And then what?" I thought.

I mulled it over some that night after I was in bed. Maybe those first few months he was just trying to make up some of what it had cost him to get me. Yet, I couldn't really believe that.

It sure hadn't seemed he was hiding anything. He'd acted and talked perfectly natural-like.

I twisted a little uneasily when I recollected how I had demanded babes from him. Well, he was sure plenty willing now, that was plain. But somehow, I wasn't. I fought shy of the very thought of it. Seemed I had to get acquainted with him all over again and there was a difference in the way I felt about him. I couldn't put my finger on it. It wasn't that I didn't like him, which I didn't very much. That had nothing to do with it. I'd married him and, of course, I expected to bear his young'uns. I'd come to it in time, I guess, but seemed I couldn't settle down to the thought just yet. I found myself twisting every which way to avoid him. And besides that, who ever heard of a woman talking to her man the way I did him? Whiskers! Wouldn't Buck just knock Becky's head off if she tried it! Yet, my man only laughed.

I couldn't figure out Skinks neither. From the way they talked I guessed they'd been friends for years. Why did Skinks stay around? Of course, he wasn't no bother, and he did spin tales of his hunting and trapping for the young'uns. He did talk to Pudge in his gibberish—French, he said it was, which pleased the little fellow. But just the same, I couldn't see he had any reason to keep staying on.

The next morning, Jim Beam sprang from the cubby and fairly leaped at me before the men come in from the barn. "What's wrong with Pa?" he demanded, "Hey, Ma! I don't like it! No, I don't! What's wrong with him, Ma?"

Well, who would ever dare to hug Jim Beam? But, oh, how I wanted to. I turned back to the pone I was making. "Don't rightly know," I decided honesty was the best policy. "Can't reckon, Jim Beam. Might be most anything. However, I do reckon all will be well. You'll just have to give him time."

He waved his hands and turned away and I wasn't sure whether Jim Beam would be silent or not. Well, that was that. Whatever would be, would be. It wasn't up to me to change nothing, even if I could.

I didn't like any part of what was going on and I kept a heavy skillet handy on the hearth or sideboard.

Maybe I was over-protective, but I had spent a winter as good as snowed-in with these young'uns. If they hadn't been mine before, they sure were mine now.

The next day, the man and Skinks started to build the extra room for sleeping the boys. The man was still brisk and sharp with the boys. I sure couldn't see how he had once told me that it seemed he didn't rightly know how to put them to work. He sure didn't have any trouble now. He kept them working from breakfast to supper and they did the chores besides.

I saw Jim Beam, leaning back, his hands braced tightly down against his hips, shouting up earnestly at his father and, I never did know, but I strongly suspected, that was why Pudge was allowed to ride Horse's neck while they dragged in the heavy logs. He picked big ones, and then had Jim Beam, Fly, and Toady help chop. When Pudge snaked them out of the woods behind Horse, they were logs. The ends were the same size, and the branches were all gone. He dragged the logs into position for Skinks.

Skinks had Chunk and Short knocking in the wedges to hold the logs. When they had done that, he marked the line with his axe, drove the wedges, and split the logs. He left the halves where they lay. Then Pudge pulled the next one in alongside.

For three days they split logs. Those days were cold, but they were dry. The man worked like a giant. I stood back and watched him. He ate the huge meals I cooked without com-ment and almost without manners. The boys ate, too. And they tumbled into bed almost as soon as they were done.

Skinks ate and he worked, but he didn't seem to change at all.

On the first night, I watched Jim Beam. He kept switching his spoon from hand to hand. I caught his wrists and turned his hands in mine. His palms and fingers were split, blistered, worn through the skin down to the flesh. Jim Beam didn't holler. I didn't like it that Jim Beam didn't holler.

I put water to heat, and I got out my dwindling supply of lard. Skinks caught my arm and leaned his head close. "Body water's best, Ma'am," he mumbled. And then he took Jim Beam outside.

I stared. I shook my head in disbelief. Maybe he was right. He was. Jim Beam's hands hardened. The word passed among the boys, and then after that, I saw no more raw hands. But I did see tired boys. They had no time to play. Not even the little ones. Their little lead soldiers lay in a heap, mixed red and blue, and they fell into the trundle with Toady, with no happy playtime at night.

It was too much. The matter of the room was not that important. A day or two didn't matter I reckoned, but the man drove hard. I set my heels and carefully counted off every six days.

The seventh day they rested, and I saw to it. I slapped my heavy bible upon the table and flipped open its pages. Seemed I was inspired like Pastor used to be back home. I read a lesson for the young'uns. Then I excused them and I held church for two hours for the man and Mr. Skinks.

Now, did I ever think that I could talk like a preacher? Well, I got all those notions knocked out of me in a hurry. I bored the man and Skinks with my sermons. I bored them stiff. The man made no bones about it. Mr. Skinks suffered in silence. And I reckon I poured it on. I was God-fearing and always reckoned any young'un ought to have the fear of the Lord put into him. But it wasn't really for the young'uns that I did this. Well, what I really meant was that the young'uns got enough religion already; however, probably the man didn't get nothing. But more importantly, it took up their time, and it prevented the man from driving the boys so hard.

I'm sure he knew what I was about. Why he gave in, I couldn't say. But he did. And that was enough for me. He grunted and grumbled. He watched me. And it cost me nearly all of the pure coffee I had hoarded away.

The store of meat in the smokehouse dwindled. Outside, it was cold and sharp, with the coming spring. Good hunting weather. The man didn't look to the gun on Jim Beam's deer horns.

He didn't give Jim Beam any time, anyway. But Jim Beam's spirits went on. He slammed open the door. "Hey! Ol' gun!" he shouted, "Hey, there! Goin' huntin' soon! Show ol' Toady how to shoot! Sure, I will! Hey, Toady! Show ya'! Sure!"

He never gave up shouting. Everything he said he shouted or yelled or hollered. It was just that he didn't shout as often as he used to. But then, he didn't need to. His Pa did it for him. He would rear back in his chair and bellow out. And always I was startled. He was looser. Seemed like his muscles strung out, his mouth laughed with an easiness that put me on guard.

His whole manner was strange to me, he seemed to court Skinks' approval, though for why I couldn't think. Was it just Skinks, or would it have been most anybody? He hadn't been that way with the Colbeys. He didn't care what they thought, and it had showed. Why should he care so much about Skinks?

Well, that didn't matter. I preached them a sermon every Sabbath and I was hard put to it to come up with the words. Reckon they wasn't rightly proper. I added anything I could think of. I stalled as innocently as I could. I acted so dumb I was surprised he didn't get angry. But he didn't. Instead, he laughed. He bellowed at Skinks, and he worked the boys hard between my rest days.

Beth worked with me and she followed me with those great big violet eyes. But she never questioned me. That hit me hard. She trusted me that I would make everything right.

And I tried. Oh, how I did try!

CHAPTER SEVENTEEN

nd so, they worked on the room to sleep the boys. They dug into the clay wall of the Square and set the ends of the half logs into the crevice. That made the joints absolutely weathertight. Skinks went to a great deal of extra work with his sharp wedges to split heavy planks to be set more than halfway down into the earth and to fashion base boards. They cut one window and no outside door.

I nodded in satisfaction. Wasn't no need for an outside door. Reckoned those boys could climb out the window faster than I could catch them at it. No sense to encourage Chunk and Short to run away any more than had to be.

The man kept on working the young'uns hard, and he didn't slight his work to make it quicker. He seemed to be taking a sly glee in the slow, but sure nearing of what he must have thought was going to be his right and just manly reward.

I studied him unbeknownst. I still had my doubts. I churned it over and over in my mind and I couldn't come up with anything that wasn't so flimsy that he would have laughed it away the instant I broached it. I sighed. When my time of reckoning came, this was going to be the one time Lucy would be ailing. I wracked my brains trying to remember all the ailments Becky had suffered to get out of her wifely duties with my brother.

And that put another thought in my mind. Was I not going to be late getting my potatoes in this year too? I'd best be at the spading. All of that would be up to me now that the young'uns were working like dogs to get that room done. I'd have only Beth's help with cutting potato eyes. Naturally, I'd want to be done before they finished the room.

One night after dinner, the man reared back in his chair and grinned. "Hey, Skinks, we'll chink the logs good and thick with clay. The roof, too, then it's done. Then we break a door through and break out the back of the fireplace. That'll give 'em heat. Reckon we make shutters for the window and that's all! Hey, Skinks! That's all!" He said it to Skinks, but he looked at me with a randy twinkle in his eye.

Well, you can just bet Lucy sure rattled her hocks. To get the thought of being with the man out of my head, I threw myself into my chores; put in half again as many potatoes as I had before. And I did it in three days! I milked Moon Eyes because Toady couldn't be spared for the chore, and I didn't have time to teach Beth. We staked her out mornings and her kids stayed close, and we brought her back into the barn in the late afternoon. The weather was getting so nice that we'd soon put Hog back into his outside pen.

Biddy pecked the yard, and her brood of pullets and the young pheasant hens began to lay. The Croaker still crowed his harsh broken cry morning and night, and he serviced them all. Leastwise, I'm sure he tried. I saved back Biddy's eggs to set her again, but as soon as the pullet eggs got good, I fried all I could gather in one morning for breakfast.

They were the first eggs I'd had in near a year and reckon the young'uns couldn't remember them at all from the way they ate.

Toady tucked his head and grinned with pleasure. Fly flashed his eyes, while Pudge danced atop his stool and boomed his little laugh. Jim Beam, as he had always done, gobbled down his first one then goggled at me.

"What's that?" he shouted.

"That's eggs," I told him.

"Hey! That's as good . . . as good as pie, pretty near! Hey, Ma! Can I have another? Where'd you get 'em, Ma?"

I smiled and gave him another, "Why, the chickens lay them, Jim Beam. They're what makes the baby chicks."

"Well, don't look like no baby chicks to me!" he shouted. "And I like 'em, Ma, I do. Yeah, I do!"

I was pleased. Chunk and Short even forgot to fight, they were so busy eating, and I saw Beth wrinkle her nose and squiggle for the first time in weeks.

The man and Skinks ate four eggs each and a whole big pot full of biscuit went with them. I mentally figured what I had left of white flour. Reckon I'd just give them pone instead of biscuit and save up a few eggs. Might be I'd try a cake in my make-shift oven pot. Yes sir! I just might.

They went on with their building and the man held to his good humor. He didn't hurry. Watching him, I slowly changed my mind though there was still something nagging at the back of my mind that I couldn't shake. I'd been wed nearly a year now, and since there was soon going to be plenty of room in the Square, reckoned it was time I was having a young'un of my own.

And I reckon that's the way it would have been, too, if it hadn't been for one thing. And when that one thing was done it cut me so deep, I wouldn't have shared that big bed with the man for anything. No, sir! Not even did it mean I would have to bed in the barn with Dan'l Skinks!

They had finished the roofing and hauled the clay to chink it all good. They cut the door through the wall into the Square. I had demanded that they put that door on the far side of the hearth and leave the ladder and plank to the cubby. That little cubby was the first safe, happy refuge Pudge had ever found, and since the man had come home, that was the only place he played his haunting music. That ladder, plank, and cubby was to be left for Pudge.

That night the man again spoke to Skinks but looked to me while talking. "Tomorrow we'll open up the fireplace and hang a plank door! And then we're done, Skinks! All done!"

I had a mighty peculiar feeling when I went to bed that night. I was used to the tiny, gentle warmth of Beth next to me. And the thought that the next night there would be the big, heavy warmth of the man beside me stirred me in an oddly contrary way. I had more than a heap of trouble going to sleep.

That was wasted time. Because it was the next morning that it happened.

They snaked in a big, short log to be split for the planks for the door. The three bigger boys had gone into the woods to help with the chopping and, of course, Pudge rode Horse's neck when they dragged it in.

I was on my way from the barn to the Square and I paused to watch.

Skinks set about the log and Fly threw off the chain from Horse's harness. Pudge stayed close against Horse's neck and turned him towards the barn. Why he did what he did, I don't know, for he hadn't done it for weeks. Maybe it was because the work was done. Anyhow, he fished in his little pocket and, sitting straight, he began to blow music upon the mouth harp.

The man strode rapidly, caught Horse's bridle with one hand, and swept Pudge down with the other. He shook the little fellow viciously. "Stop making that ungodly noise, ya' gypsy bastard imp!" he roared, and then snatched Pudge's mouth harp out of his tiny hands and flung it away with all his strength.

Pudge must have been wild with fear. He shrieked in a way that wasn't even human and crouched against the ground. He put those arms up again to protect his handsome head.

That's all it took for me. I flung my apron full of eggs every which way and ran as I hadn't done since the first time I'd seen Pudge. I caught him up the way I had then and covered him with my apron as I had done before, rocking him gently to sooth his abused, gentle soul.

Immediately after, I turned to the man, and if there had been any weapon to hand, I would have killed him on the spot. Luckily, this time, I was so breathless from rage, my tongue couldn't run away with my wits. I don't know what my face looked like, but it must have been awful because the man just stood there and stared.

I looked past him to where Skinks and the other boys stood. They had seen it all. Now they waited to see what I would do. I felt Beth come up behind me and grasp my skirt.

I tried to quiet my breathing, and I tried to soothe the quivering little Pudge. I waved a hand at the boys. "All right, boys! All of you get out yonder and find your brother's mouth harp, and don't come back without it!"

They stared, waiting to see what the man would do.

But he just stood there as well, looking at me, waiting to see how this would play out.

"Hop to it!" I hollered to the young'uns as loud as I could, which was some. "Move it, right now!"

They immediately scattered. Spreading out in the direction that the harp could've gone.

I narrowed my eyes back at the man, full of rage and fury.

The man shifted from one foot to the other and opened his mouth to speak. But before he could get out a word, Skinks sidled up and forestalled whatever he was about to say, "Reckon, it's about time, Roan. We need to get our business done, and then I'll be movin' on." Skinks threw it out flat-like and dry.

I suspect Skinks was a lot of things, but one thing he wasn't. He wasn't afraid of the man.

The man gaped and there again was that Jim Beam look to him, "What do ya' mean, Skinks? You agreed we'd wait till the room was done. Near got the room done! Why don't we wait a spell? Where's the harm? Hey, Skinks?"

Skinks looked at the young'uns, looked me, and then wrinkled his brow at the man, "I been partnerin' with ya' a long time, Roan Shields. I've been patient. Now it's time to complete our business, Roan. Right now."

"Few days won't make no difference, Dan'l."

"Yes, I reckon it will. There's still good huntin' up north. Will be for some time yet. If I start now, I'll make it through the season fine. But I need a place to come back to. *My place.*"

His place? What the heck was Skinks talking about?

The man turned fiery eyes on me, leveling the blame for Skinks' sudden decision squarely on my shoulders. "Ya' damned contrary woman!" he snarled.

How dare he? When it was him that lashed out at Pudge in the first place and caused Skinks to cut short whatever it was they had cooked up. I bristled out all over.

"You're mean, Roan Shields!" I snarled, "The meanest man I ever laid eyes on! You're no better than a. . .a . . . a snake, and I'll never be a true wife to the likes of you!"

The man's face went all blank. I turned on my heel and I went back into the Square Heap with Pudge shivering in my arms and his face and his tiny hands a-fire against my neck. Every step I took gave me strength. It was true. I would punish the man in every way I could, and I had learned ways enough from my sister-in-law Becky to last a lifetime!

I rocked Pudge back and forth on the stool, quieting him aimlessly. I wasn't foolish enough to think that was all there was going to be to it. Not after what I'd said! I reckoned he'd do something real harsh now. We weren't meandering down the garden path so to speak. You best be ready to do more than toss roses with thorns, Lucy.

Pudge finally quieted just as Chunk and Short burst through the door. One of them carried Pudge's mouth harp in an outstretched hand.

I took it, knocked out the dirt it had gathered against the hearth wall and let down my apron to wipe it well. I'm not given to demonstrating my feelings much, but it was different when it came to Pudge. I gently put the harp into Pudge's tiny hands and turned him out of my lap.

Beth caught him. She smoothed his rumpled hair and kissed his brow. She set his feet on the first ladder rung up to the cubby. He skittered up a few steps then hung by one arm to look down on her. She smiled and waved him upward.

Of course, he went. Any one of them would have. I was the woman, and Beth was an extension of me. I was Ma. I was protection and security. I was a female animal defending her young. They were animal young depending on me. Even against their own sire!

Well, that was all it took for me. Should the man decide to resort to strength, he would not find me without resources. I would fight with any weapon in hand, be it skillet or my own body.

Which is exactly what I thought when I heard a knock at the front door. I grabbed a skillet and opened the door expecting to lock horns with the man—just how much it would be was unknown. But instead, there in the doorway, stood an unknown older man, and two younger men on either side of him.

I must've looked like they'd just slapped me upside the head with a dead rabbit. Because the older man said, "Whoa, whoa ma'am. We mean no harm to you. We're just neighbors from a few homesteads over."

I softened my face and put down the skillet. "I'm sorry. I didn't mean to be an unfriendly neighbor," I said warily, "What can I do you for?"

"I'm Monroe Chestly and these here are my sons, Edgar and Quentin. We're lookin' for Roan Shields.

"My husband? What do you need with him?"

Monroe Chestly looked at Beth staring out from behind me, her eyes wide with concern.

"Um, it's men's business, ma'am. Do you know where I can find him?"

Normally, I wouldn't be in a right mind to just let strangers roam the property looking for the man, but I was so mad at him, I thought it'd do the man good to get a good tongue lashing by someone who weren't me.

"Last I saw him, he was heading toward the barn," I told Monroe Chestly.

"Mind if we go find him, Mrs. Shields?" Monroe asked.

"Go right ahead," I replied.

And with that, the three men headed off in the direction of the barn. I shut the door before they got to the barn door.

Shortly after that, I started making supper. But by the time I had the boys call the man and Skinks to come in and eat, they were gone.

"What do you mean, they're gone?" I asked Jim Beam

"I can't find them anywhere, Ma."

"Did you look in the field?"

"I looked everywhere, Ma. We all did. They're gone."

And so it was, Skinks and the man had vanished. I don't know if it had anything to do with Monroe Chestly and his brood, but I never saw hide nor hair of them after that. Well, not until much, much later.

For the moment, I was stung with hurt. How did he dare to just walk off like that? This was his place—his young'uns!

In the blink of an eye, I realized I had brought this onto myself. I had declared myself against him. Why did I expect anything else? Why shouldn't he leave? Me, with my big mouth. I had given him leave to go. Yeah, I had. Shoot, Lucy, you got what you asked for . . . again!

I didn't dwell on it. What's the use? We still needed to finish that room, which would be tricky without the man and Skinks. But with the young'un's help, I knocked a hole in the back of the fire wall. It wasn't neat, but it would serve. I left the log to lay. The slab door wasn't important.

I stepped in through the rough-cut doorway. It was a fine room. It would work, but there weren't any beds and nothing to make them out of. I shook my head. Good thing the warm weather was coming up. The gaping room took away lots of our warmth from the fireplace.

Well, best just to leave things be as they were for now. Better turn your mind to the fields, Lucy, and how they were going to get planted. Or, leastwise, how the ones we had seed for were to be planted. It would take more time, working without the man. Reckon we'd best start plowing early.

There was the rest of my truck garden to put in, but there really wasn't any reason to dress out the pheasant pullets yet. They could be killed as we needed them. I guessed they'd be mostly stewed anyhow, what with the time I'd have to spend in the fields, not to mention the chores like washing and such that was far and away too heavy for Beth's little hands. Might be we'd even get to where we'd be down to Beth's soggy grits. Well, no, we wouldn't go that far, but I could put on the great pot of stew and leave Beth to watch it. Was time she learned how to make pone anyway.

It really wasn't no use, but I fell to fretting about Hog. He'd have to be butchered out come fall and much as I'd have liked some of his side-meat and the lard from the rendering, never mind the chitlins for the young 'uns to chew on, I just couldn't figure how we could butcher him. I didn't know how to stick a hog. And, even if I managed that, how could we hang him to gut and skin and would I be strong enough to cut him up, right or wrong? Kind of daft-like, I wondered if we could drive him into the smokehouse? No, that wouldn't work. We'd have a pool of blood where the fire was supposed to be and Hog still wouldn't be hung, gutted, nor skinned. Besides, we'd lose all the lard!

No, it wouldn't do. Mr. Colbey crossed my mind, but I shook my head. Nope! I reckon I'd keep on feeding Hog 'til he was a hundred before I asked for help I couldn't pay for from the Colbeys.

I thought of the scant bit of gold left in my trunk. I couldn't spend that! I sure wouldn't give it to the Colbeys! We might need it bad one day.

I put Hog out of my mind. First things first, and there was plenty to do before fall. The supply of staples in the pantry would run out before winter. Well, Fly would come in handy. We'd grind our oats like the Indians did. We'd eat oat cakes. And we'd shell and grind our own corn. I'd set Biddy again with as many eggs as she could take. I'd keep a few pullets for laying.

I could butcher out Moon Eyes' kids. No! The Nanny, maybe, but not the Billy! And we'd have milk a good long while yet.

We'd make it, though. Sure we would. And next year the boys would be a year bigger. And each year they'd be bigger still and stronger, and one day soon there would be enough men to make a fine farm out of the Square.

Yes, we'd make out. We'd have six fine, strong men on the Square one day. This thought so relieved my mind that I flung caution to the winds and I baked that cake. It came out high and light and smelled up the whole house.

Beth swooped Tildy from the bed and sat on a stool by the hearth and rocked and petted her doll while she wrinkled her nose and squiggled. Way down deep it sure made me feel good.

I had the cake out and cooling on the sideboard and supper near ready when the boys came in. Jim Beam slammed the door back as he hadn't done in some time.

"Hey, Ma!" he yelled, "Hey, Beth! Look at that! Look at that dumb ol' Lost Be! Never seen nothin' like that before! Bet you didn't either! Bet ya'! Hey, Ma? Can we go hunting tomorrow? Show ol' Toady how to shoot? Hey, Ma?"

I nodded at him as I lifted the pail of milk from Moon Eyes, evening milking that Toady brought me. I looked up and there was Lost Be all bedecked with straw and flowers. I shook my head and smiled.

Fly slid in, his eyes shining, and Chunk and Short tumbled after squabbling. Pudge was the only one who sidled in quietly and flashed his eyes around the room, grinning.

Jim Beam thrust his nose up, wrinkled it, and sniffed loudly. "What's that?" he hollered.

That set all the other boys to sniffing, noses in the air. I quirked my lips, "That's cake," I told them. "It's for after supper, but nobody gets any if they don't wash up."

They set to washing in the pantry and Beth giggled and pulled the wide woven hay collar off Lost Be. Don't reckon the dog really cared much about that. It was the bands the boys had put around her ankles that worried her. She stepped high for all the world like she was walking on eggs. Beth stripped them away. Lost Be was so pleased that she galumphed around like she was a tiny pup and bonked her head under the table. Then she dashed out the door and set up a needless clatter in the yard.

Looked like Lost Be was relieved the man was gone, too.

Beth and I took our stools back and even Jim Beam didn't jaw Fly when he took the man's place.

Supper was near like a party that night. I didn't have any icing for the cake, but they ate it all at that one sitting. I smiled to see Fly pitch in and get his fair share. Pudge relaxed too and leaped atop his stool three times during the two great chunks he ate. Even Lost Be got cake.

The man's being here had tightened up on my nerves for some reason, but I didn't realize just how finely wound I had been until he was gone. And I didn't have to stand those too-wise eyes of Dan'l Skinks!

My heart was feather light.

Chapter Eighteen

I reckon it did some sinking in the next morning when I got up and looked around me, but I took a big breath and squared my shoulders. It was going to take more than a man like Roan Shields to beat me and this posse of young'uns.

The boys scattered to take care of the animals. I raided the smoke house for breakfast meat.

It was near empty. One, maybe two, more meals.

Beth and I cleared away after we had all eaten, and I fetched the powder and shot.

Jim Beam's face brightened. He took the fixings and, before I knew it, he had Toady measuring powder for him. Fly sat back and smiled. Pudge sat with his wee feet dangling over the edge of the cubby and played his eerie music softly.

"You take Toady and Fly," I told Jim Beam. "We've got to save on shot, Jim Beam. And make sure you bring home all the leftovers. Hear?"

He nodded, but he was taken up with telling and showing Toady. I left him be. He'd always brought back the powder and shot he didn't use. Reckon he would this time too.

Pudge went to the barn. I shook my head. Our wild little Pudge would never make a hunter. All his tenderness was with the wild things. I watched and I whispered to Beth and she took Pudge and Lost Be to look for poke sallet greens about the time the other boys should come in.

Chunk and Short resorted to fists near the well. One maintained their brothers would come back with no less than a bear, and the other held out for a deer. I smiled and let them go at it.

Wasn't long after Beth and Pudge had gone before Toady came in. He led Horse out. "They got something!" he declared about his brothers as hunters.

I gathered my wet hands in my apron and ran after him. "Whatever it is, tell Fly to dress it out," I shouted at him, "I want it to look like meat when you bring it in!"

He waved a hand, but didn't stop. Nonetheless, it was a dressed-out deer they brought back. Don't know how Fly prevailed over Jim Beam about the horns, but he did.

That wasn't practical, nor really fair maybe, but I couldn't bear to have Pudge hurt any more just then. Of course, he would realize one day, but right now he had had more than his share of hard knocks without having too many night-mares about the food he ate. Fly had cut it across the loins making two pieces. We hung it in the smoke house, and I hacked out a good chunk to carry to the house.

I left Beth to redd up after dinner, with the help of the twins, and took the older boys to spade the truck garden. We had to have the food. My pantry shelves would be empty by the time the garden began to bear. I thanked my stars that I had had the foresight to save extra seed. The garden patch was to be half again as big this year. There were more mouths to feed now. And there was just me to do it.

I sunk the spade and turned the fresh earth. Tomorrow we would start to plow the fields.

I would have to watch ol' Horse. I'd have to be careful not to work him too hard and feed him good. He must pull the plow down every row we turned. I could sink the plow and hold it straight, but I couldn't plow all the fields we had seed for. It would take at least two of the bigger boys and maybe all three to even sink the plow. Pudge would have to ride Horse's neck and keep the furrows straight.

What was it the man had said before he left the first time? Spread out. Plant the fallow field. It would take us a long time. It would take all of us working together to get through the coming winter. I paused, wiped my damp brow and cast my eye over the boys.

Jim Beam turned a spade of earth. "Hey! Look at that! Look at all them fishin' worms! Hey, Fly! Hey, Toady an' Pudge! Look at 'em all! Can we go fishin', Ma? Hey, Ma? Can we?"

All their faces swiveled toward me. I didn't even pause to think before I answered. And when I thought about it later, I was glad I was bound by my word. They worked so hard; they deserved something.

"On the Sabbath, Jim Beam. On the Sabbath," I pledged.

Fly's eyes glittered and he leaned on the handle of the shovel for a minute.

"Can't dig 'em now, Jim Beam!" Toady cried, "They'll die! Can't do it!"

"I deeg, Jeem!" Pudge shrieked, "I deeg!"

"Yeah!" Jim Beam danced in the soft dirt, "Yeah! We'll all dig 'em, come Sunday! Yeah! Sunday! And we'll go fishin' and I guess we'll catch a hundred of 'em! Yeah! A hundred!"

Yes, I reckoned they would. If they didn't catch a hundred, they'd catch ten and it would be just as good. It wasn't really about how many they caught, nor whether they caught any. It was the going fishing that counted.

The next day, I left Fly in command of Beth and the twins to begin the planting. Apparently, the moon didn't concern itself with our problems and so Beth got her wish. They planted the beans first. It was several days before the dark of the moon.

I put Pudge astride Horse's neck, and he was entirely happy. I plowed that entire day while Jim Beam seeded and Toady covered behind me. I got well ahead of them, and that was good.

I had all of them working behind me the next day. Beth followed my instructions faithfully and gave us a simple but filling dinner. I quit before sunset to rest Horse and to cook.

The next day, the three eldest boys laid their weight on the plow, and it was all they could manage. We took turns. I plowed one day, the boys the next, and five days later we were all completely exhausted, but we had planted the field that had taken us three days to plant with the man's help.

It was the Sabbath. We rested. I held off my bible reading until after supper because the boys went fishing. They caught a mess of fish, and we ate them avidly.

When the young'uns were all abed, I sat before the fire with my hands idle for the first time since I'd been big enough to work. I must have been entirely tired and completely at ease, for I saw in fantasy the boys as men walking my fields. I saw Beth as a beautiful young woman with a babe at her breast.

I shook myself sharply. Do not dream away these precious, terrible years, Lucy. Be content with what you have while you have it. If you live ahead of time, there is little left to savor when you have reached that future.

It took us seven days more to put the fallow field to corn. I shook my head. I didn't see how we could go on. We were exhausted. Wash backlogged. My sideboard in the kitchen began to look like Lizbeth's had. I eyed the huge pot with horror, expecting at any time to lift its lid and see Beth's drowned, greasy grits. Never had I been so bone-weary.

There were still three fields to go. The rye for money. The oats and the hay for the animals. There was all of the hoeing, there was all of the reaping, and the processing afterwards. Tears dampened my eyes for the first time I could remember.

But I drew a deep breath, and I set my teeth. I couldn't quit. The eyes of the young'uns made me keep going. I would drop in my tracks before I would quit. And if I dropped, I'd die.

But I wouldn't quit!

We had started the third field. The oats. I was some six hours into my plowing, plodding along deadly behind Horse and Pudge, when I suddenly became aware that Jim Beam was running across the deep gouged ruts shouting at the top of his lungs.

I shook my head. I could see him. I "whoa-ed" the horse. I could hear him, but his words made no sense. He might as well have been Pudge, shrieking his gibberish at me. I stared dully at him. I was conscious that the other young'uns were converging on me from their places. Jim Beam stood at the plow handle and shouted up at me. My eyes fled from face to face, and they all shrieked at me. I sought the shape of Beth's face. "Pa's here," she said. I don't know if she shouted it or if she whispered.

Strength shot through me. I dug the plow deep and I lifted my head. He was coming. Down he strode across the fields, lurching when he hit the plowed ruts. His shoulders swung and my head swirled. I clung tightly against the plow handles, and I watched him swing on and on, nearer and nearer.

He grasped my shoulders, "Lucy! Oh, Lucy! I told you I'd be back. Why'd you start this? There's time. There's plenty of time yet for planting."

Well now, that just showed how much he knew. I straightened and struck his hand away.

"There isn't any time!" I shouted at him. "Not when me and the young'uns have to do it alone! You left with Skinks, and I reckon you can just go back to him! Don't need you! Don't want you! And you're not beating nor scaring none of my children! Never again! And now how do you like that, Roan Shields?"

He pulled his hands back, "Why I reckon that's alright, Lucy. I wasn't aiming to beat no young'uns nor scare none neither. And what's this about Skinks? What's wrong with you, Lucy?"

"Nothing, Mr. Shields! Nothing at all!" I screamed, "Only just you can't beat and scare Pudge like you did! You can't order Toady out! You can't shame Fly! You can't ignore Beth! Nor the twins! And you can't buy me, Mr. Roan Shields, with no half-built room!"

His face blanched. He took a step backwards, "Lucy! What are you talking about? What do you mean? What half built room?"

"The one you thought you could use to buy me into doing . . . ," I was so mad, I could barely breath. All of a sudden my anger spilled out of me like cistern overflowing in a rain storm. "All this time, I'm begging you for babes, and nothing! Throwing myself at you like... I don't know what. But then you go and treat me like some whore who does easy favors just for . . . ."

"Lucy! You shut your mouth! Now!" the man bellowed in my face.

I was as stunned by his outburst as if he had lifted a hand to me.

"If you ever speak to me like that again, I *will* beat you—beat you good! You hear me, Lucy?"

I immediately backed down, still reeling that he actually fought back. Dazed, I nodded. I heard. I understood. He'd got rid of Dan'l Skinks and he seemed to be back—back to his old self, the man I married.

"Now go inside and put a meal on the table, do you hear me?" he commanded.

I obliged, glad that he was *really* back to his old self. I cooked. You bet I did. And Beth scuttled, seeming to know all I wanted before I asked.

Once the man came inside, the young'uns were wary of him at first, too. But when he tousled the twins upon my bed and played roughly with Lost Be, who behaved as though she had no mind at all, everyone heaved a sigh of relief. He talked fishing and hunting with Jim Beam and Toady, and was patient in listening to their long, drawn-out tales. He questioned Fly about Howl-of-the-Wolf and nodded solemnly. He caught up Beth and kissed her soundly, and he perched Pudge upon his knee gently. Pudge was cautious at first, but then soon felt safe enough to bellow his husky little laugh and spout his gibberish, which seemed mostly directed at me. I smiled and waved my hands at him. Of course, I couldn't understand his words.

But I didn't have to, Pudge's trust and sentiment was loud and clear. The man lifted Pudge, and the little boy gave himself gladly. He was not afraid. He held back nothing. That satisfied me. Whatever the problem the man had had with Skinks, and maybe even the neighbor men, had apparently been settled. My man was back, *alone*. He was as I had first known him.

He checked out the empty room and shook his head at the uneven hole in the back of the fireplace. He squatted and talked seriously with the boys, nodding his head grimly, while Beth and I readied up the house for bedtime. Once the young'uns were asleep, he asked me a lot of questions about the new room, about how he had acted, when he came and went, about Skinks, and even about the visiting neighbor men. I answered as truthfully as I knew how, but in return he offered no answers. Even when I asked questions.

Then he retired to his own bed in the barn hayloft, with no further word from me. Although he never denied anything the young'uns and I had said about how he acted before, I felt in my heart he knew more than he was sayin'. But that made no-never-mind to me. All I cared about was that the man was back the way I remembered him best. How that happened didn't matter.

We all bedded down early. Tomorrow was another day.

Chapter Nineteen

Indeed, it was. The man plunked down my small leather poke before his plate the next morning. "There, Lucy, I expect you worked harder for it than me," he upended it with his big fingers and dumped a pile of gold pieces to the tabletop.

I stared at it. I didn't know if it was a good winter's work or not. None of my brothers had ever hunted or trapped for pelts for a full winter.

"It's enough to do all we have to do, plus a nest egg to spare for winter. We can get the mule we need, and since you got the plowing near half done, I reckon that I'll just clear more land and put another field to rye this spring. Which means I won't even have to go trapping next winter."

I nodded. This was what I had expected from him when he had just come back with Skinks.

Sure, Skinks had to be the trouble. There was something more than met the eye in that friendship. I dared a question, "What did you do with Skinks?"

He looked at me while he mulled that over, then he answered easily, "I reckon, I do know Dan'l Skinks. He's probably trapping up north this very minute. Nothing can keep Dan'l out of the woods for long."

That was all he gave me. I let the memory of those last few weeks slide out of my mind. He wasn't going to explain it all to me, and it didn't matter. He was here as he had been in the beginning, and he wasn't making plans to leave again. That was enough for me.

He got up, dug into his pocket and smiled at the young'uns. Not that loose quick grin, but a slow smile that showed he really did care about them.

"I brought you all presents," he told them, and while they all stared wide-eyed, he put a silver dollar into the hands of each one.

They sure made a commotion. They all talked at the same time at first, but after a while. one-by-one they began to tell what they would do with the money.

Pudge leaped atop his stool and shrieked he would give his to Horse and he didn't care that everyone laughed. Toady shyly averred that he'd save his up against Christmas. Beth nodded her agreement. The twins reckoned they'd buy more soldiers so they could really have a big battle and Jim Beam shouted that next time we went to town. he was going to buy and eat a whole dollar's worth of peppermint sticks. Fly silently tucked his away in his little leather pouch. He didn't need to say that his was for Howl-of-the-Wolf.

The man looked again to me. "I don't reckon we ought to plow Horse for a couple of days. Let him rest. Instead, we'll go to town to get the mule. Is there something you need. too, Lucy?"

I flat-faced him, "Why, I think we might as well all go along," I answered.

He nodded, "Why not." He drained his cup, chinked it to the table, and stretched.

I jerked my eyes away, but I could feel the heat in my face as the blood came up. This was sure not the time for that! Not after what I'd shouted at him in front of Dan'l Skinks.

That day, he chinked out the hole in the back of the hearth so it was even. He built a shutter for the one window. He stood in the middle of the floor in the new room and stared at the blank side wall. "You should have left another window," he muttered and shook his head.

"You said it'd be too cold in winter," I reminded him.

He stared at me, "Yeah, that's true, but it's gonna be hot in the summer."

"No matter. None of the boys will be sleepin' in here this summer. There's nothing for them to sleep on," I told him tartly.

His eyes softened and his lips quirked, "There's no reason we can't fetch the trundle in here. And Fly's cot. That'll spread them out a little, Lucy. And I can take Jim Beam and Pudge in the barn with me."

"No!" I made it sharp, "Not Pudge!"

He stared at me a long time. "I reckon you're right, Lucy. Best to leave Pudge and Jim Beam be till we can get a bed for them."

He moved the trundle and Fly's cot, though, to the new room, and I have to admit it sure made more room. He set the three eldest boys to whittling pegs, which he drove into the wall to hang their clothes.

They drove Hog into his outside pen and Jim Beam poured him a couple of buckets of water. Hog had a good wallow, and it was plain to see he enjoyed it.

We started staking out the kids along with Moon Eyes, and I had to smile every time my eyes crossed the little Nanny. Make a good milker, she would, in time, now that we wouldn't have to eat her. I decided to set a few eggs from the pheasant hens just to see what a cross between a chicken and pheasant would look like.

Next day, we went to town again, and this time, we had two more young'uns. Chunk and Short hadn't ever been before and their eyes bugged out. In spite of all that had been planned for the spending of the silver dollars, nary a one left its resting place.

I fortified my dwindled supply of materials, thread, needles, pins, and yarn. Spring would not leave much time for sewing, yet there would have to be some. Seven young'uns! And young'uns never been known to stop growing just because it was planting time. I ordered food staples carefully, my one luxury being coffee. When the man laid the gold upon the counter to pay for it, he added a little box of tea for me, and peppermint sticks all around. Silly, a grown man and woman sucking on peppermint sticks. Maybe, but that was the best peppermint I had ever tasted.

It wasn't my place to ask the man how much he had paid for the mule he got, so I didn't. It was a fine mule. A great bay with huge ears, a velvety nose, and an ornery way of showing his teeth.

Big-mouth Lucy did it again. It popped out before I thought about it, "He looks like Dan'l Skinks," and then I had to stick up my chin, but I could feel the color hot in my face.

The man turned away, his mouth twitching suspiciously, and Jim Beam took up my words and shouted them out for the whole town to hear. "Hey, Ma! Whoo-eee! Does! Looks just like ol' Mr. Skinks! Hey, Fly! Ol' Mule does! Hey, Toady! Hey, Pudge! Hey, Pa! Don't he? Yeah! Yeah, he does!"

And that's how the mule came to be called Dan. Of course, it started out as "Old Mr. Dan'l Skinks," but that didn't last until we got home. So, Dan he was.

The man tied him behind the wagon and Pudge scrunched down against the tailgate and watched him with shining eyes. Beautiful little Pudge now had two loves, and that was nearly as good as the man having a strong young animal to pull the plow and draw the wagon.

The next day, the man plowed the fields with the help of the older boys, and I set about catching up with my chores around the house with the help of Beth and the twins.

I set the twins to hoeing in my truck garden, and half the time they hoed and half the time they fought.

Beth and I scrubbed and scoured, and again I was ashamed that my sideboard and pantry shelves were nearly as dirty as Lizbeth's had been.

I washed all the clothes I could find, and I cooked. I cooked everything good I could think of. At dinnertime Chunk and Short carried food to the man and the other boys in the field.

After supper that night, the man sat quiet, his huge arms propped on the table, and listened to Pudge's poignant music for a while before he took his way to the barn loft.

I laid myself down with a good tiredness and many plans for the next day.

I didn't sleep long. I don't know how long, but when I lifted myself on my elbow at Lost Be's persistent, low growling, there was enough light from the banked fire in the hearth for me to see the stealthy wiggling of the door latch.

The man! Something was wrong! Maybe he was ill!

I sprang up, shushed Lost Be softly and slipped the bolt. I swung open the door and came nearer to fainting than I ever had before in my life.

He pressed forward and I gave way for him. "I've got to talk to ya', Missus. It's important! I've got to."

I caught up the lamp, took a light on a straw from an ember, and set it against the wick. It sprang into flame, and I turned with my heart pounding in my throat. "Dan'l Skinks! What are you doing here?" I asked in a loud whisper.

"Ya'd best to keep yer voice down," he cautioned, and he edged forward to clamp his hand on the edge of the table. "Best not to wake the young'uns. Don't be scared, Mrs. Shields. I'm not here to harm you."

"I'm not afraid of you!" I snapped. "What do you want, Skinks?"

"I've got to talk to ya', Mrs. Shields. It's about Roan. He . . . ," he broke off shortly. "Can I have a cup of water?"

I fetched the dipper. He drank and I prodded him, "Go on."

"Well, Mrs. Shields, I hate to do this, but ya' got to know. Ya' see, Roan, he . . . . ."

"Skinks!"

Skinks spun around, and there, in the doorway, stood the man. His feet were bare, so he made no sound as he crept up on us. Skinks looked like he'd seen a ghost, dropping his water cup at the sight of the man.

I don't know what I expected. I don't hardly know what I saw or heard. But I stood there dumbly watching and listening.

After a second, Skinks got ahold of himself and stared at the man through narrowed eyes.

"Morgan?" Skinks choked. "Is that you?" He gulped at his own realization.

"What are you doing skulking round here in the dead of night, Dan'l?" demanded the man. His voice was harsh.

"Ain't skulkin'!" Skinks slid down on a stool and ran his hand over his face. He stared at the man and shook his head.

"Dang me for a pure fool, Morgan. I shoulda figured it out that it was you! I shoulda! Woulda gone straight to the barn if I'd a-knowed."

"Knowed what?" the man asked.

"Knowed you was here. And that she was your woman. Knowed Roan was a-lyin' his damn head off, like usual!"

The man sat down on a stool facing Skinks and shoveled his fingers through his hair. All of a sudden, his face was tired, "He's not with you now, is he?"

Skinks shook his head, "No he ain't. Never ever comin' back neither. You're rid of Roan Shields for good, Morgan. That's what I came to tell Miz Shields."

The man closed his hands into fists and put them knuckle to knuckle before him on the table. "Tell her? What for?" he asked quietly.

Skinks stared, "'Cause I believed she was Roan's wife! That's what he told me when we showed up. I came back because I figured her and that passel of young'uns would be a-settin' here a-waitin' on him and I . . . ."

"A-waitin' on him!?" The man barked out that short, unfunny laugh, "What for? Dan'l, you're a damn fool! You've been partners with Roan fer years. You know he's not about to settle nowheres long enough to do no good. Killed Lizbeth, he did, leaving her on this place alone with two young'uns. She couldn't make it, Lizbeth couldn't. She wrote me after Roan left, Dan'l. Did you know that? Did Roan know that? No! You betcha he didn't! When I came to help Lizbeth, folks just figured that I was Roan come back—and I let them think that. You know why Dan'l? Because I had to stay. Because Lizbeth was dyin'! And the young'uns were . . . ." The man lowered his head at the memory, "I swear to God, if Roan would have been here, I would have killed him!"

"Morg," Skinks said softly, "I didn't know it. I wouldn't a-come here with him if I'd a-known that."

"I knew he'd been here. I knew it the minute I came back. Even before Lucy and the young'uns told me."

My hair hung loose around me. I pushed it back from my face. What were they talking about? I was Mrs. Roan Shields, wasn't I? And yet, plain as plain, the man was not Roan Shields, but someone named Morgan. The man who had built the room to sleep the boys was Roan Shields. And yet they were the same man. *Weren't they?* I had eyes to see with! I shook my head and their voices came through again.

"That's why I came back, Morg," Skinks said. "I thought she was Roan's woman. She never denied it and he swore it was true. It warn't none of my business, even though it went against the grain with me."

The man looked at me with sad eyes. "Did he . . . . Did you and him . . . ."

"No!" I said quickly!

The man looked relieved. Then he turned his attention back to Skinks, "And now you're saying he's dead." It was a statement, not a question.

"Ain't no doubt about that! I seen it happen. All of us told old Roan it was gonna happen someday, him bein' the way he was about wimmin."

"A husband?"

"Naw! A pa and two brothers."

"Monroe Chestly. And his sons," I added.

Skinks looked at me surprised, "Right true, ma'am. How did you know?"

"They came here looking for 'Mr. Shields.' Didn't tell me why. Said they had *'men's business'* with him."

"That they did, ma'am." Then to the man he added, "She was short 'n' sweet, Morg. Just sixteen, the gal was. When she told Roan she was in a family way, he laughed at her and took off, never expectin' to see her ever again. Seems after that, the gal, she killed herself. From then on, the pa and her brothers been hellbent on making Roan pay for what he done. They've been huntin' old Roan for the better part of a year. When they showed up here, Roan saw them before they saw him and took off. Morg, they blew him to bits with three sawed-off shot guns when they finally caught up to him."

The man shook his head, "I can't grieve for him, Dan'l, I can't. Brother or no."

They surely reckoned I'd gone suddenly daft. I dashed to the corner where my trunk was, and I rummaged madly through it until I came up with my marriage paper. I tipped it to the firelight to read it. Somewhere deep inside me a small warmth started. It swelled and grew into such happiness that I felt I would burst. There were two men! Not just brothers. Twins! On paper I thought I was married to . . . the dead one. But in reality, I was married to *Morgan Shields*—the one who cared for his family. Or rather his brother's family.

"We have another issue to discuss, Morgan." Skinks' tone suddenly became all business. "Roan owed me money. A gambling debt to the tune of $2,000. He done run out on me, too. But when I caught up with him, I wouldn't let him outta my sight until he paid me. That's why I showed up here with him."

"Roan didn't have any money," the man said flatly.

"No he didn't. But he did have this land. This farm, which he agreed to sign over to me to pay off his debt. Now that he's dead, that debt rolls over to his wife, Mrs. Shields," Skinks looked at me like he expended me to get out my purse.

"What?" My mouth gaped open, and my head spun with what was happening. Did I really owe Skinks $2,000?

"She isn't married to Roan, she's married to me," declared the man with so much conviction, he made me feel safe for the first time in a long time. "Roan wasn't married, so this land, our family's land, rolls over to me. I am his heir, his next of kin."

"Then I guess *you* owe me money, Morgan," Skinks puffed out his chest like a proud banker.

"Roan's debt died with Roan," the man replied with confidence. He stood up and squared off against Skinks, letting the little man know that he was ready for a fight, if need be. "Nobody is taking this land from me, from my wife, or from my family," he said sharply.

I joined the man, shoulder to shoulder, to let him know that we were as one. Instinctively, I took his hand. It was the first time I had touched him intentionally, but it came real easy.

I guess it did to him too, for he took my hand, and squeezed it tight.

In that moment, Skinks knew immediately that he was outmatched.

The next day, we moved Jim Beam and Toady to the man's old hayloft bed in the barn. That's where they'd be sleeping for now on, 'cause we needed Fly's cot for Beth. Yes, Lucy Shields was finally about to start to work on a babe of her own, with a man that she had grown to care for.

The man never fully explained anything to me. I knew he wouldn't. He knew there was no need. Roan Shields was dead. The man I had married, the man who was here with me now was Morgan Shields, his twin brother. And I had Chunk and Short to prove it.

And the rest of the young'uns? Well, didn't make no never-mind that they weren't his. Nor mine. They were ours. And always would be.

Epilogue

And so the time passed, and life at the Square Heap continued to be a mix of hard work and simple rewards. Springtime melted into summer, summer ended, winter came and went, each season bringing with it a new and exciting chapter in our lives. All the heartache and insecurity of the past two years was gone and mostly forgotten.

I have a baby daughter of my own now. Augusta, we call her "Gussie," who toddles about the place, adored by her Ma and Pa, her brothers, and especially Beth, who revels in having a live baby doll to care for and love. And, although I have not told Morgan yet, there is to be another addition to the Shields clan by Christmas.

Flying Cloud headed back to his village to sit at the knee of Howl-of-the-Wolf and learn how to be the chieftain of his mother's people someday. He is a fine, strong, brave young man now. How much longer he will "come home" to us, we do not know, but he will always be welcomed and loved.

Jim Beam still raises the roof with his shouts and commotion, but as the eldest of the Shields brood, he commands a high degree of respect and loyalty from his brothers, most of the time.

Pudge remains Pudge. His understanding of American language has improved greatly, though he speaks with a sweet, melodious accent. He is mercurial, quick, and agile despite his physical impediments, a true sprite of a child who loves all the animals on the place, ol' Horse and Dan the mule, most of all. And he still speaks his French gibberish to them.

The twins? Well, they are still young, but they adore Morgan as much as they resemble him and follow in his footsteps with dogged concentration. They still fight with each other, or back-to-back against their brothers, whenever the spirit moves them, for any reason that serves, or for no reason at all.

Toady Wooten is still a part of our family. He works alongside Morgan as a sort of foreman of the crew, handing out duties and teaching the youngsters to share and participate in both the work and the rewards. I have often spied him leaning on a rake or shovel, lost in the vision of Beth going about her chores or playing with the baby. She is growing into a lovely and graceful woman-child. All I can do is shake my head and sigh. I guess what will be will be.

Overall, we are about as happy as a family could be. A farm that is becoming prosperous and bountiful, with a passel of healthy young'uns, and a loving and contented husband and wife working together to make it so.

If you stood and sighted down the side wall of the Square Heap, it is plain to see that the room built to sleep the boys isn't quite straight. But that makes next to no difference. It was really never square anyhow. And that's not here nor there neither. It always has been, and to me it always will be, the Square Heap.

The End

About the Author

Dora Lee McKee was born in Oklahoma in 1920 and moved to Southern California in the late 20s with her family. She was the middle daughter in a close-knit family of three girls, and attended Burbank High School, graduating in 1938.

Dora was vivacious, sociable, and a talented artist. During the early years of World War II, she worked at Lockheed as a "Rosie the Riveter." A petite woman, it was often Dora's job to rivet the nosecones onto fighter planes because she was the only person on the line small enough to get into the tight spaces with a rivet gun.

In 1945, she went to New York to visit her aunt, where she unexpectedly met and married a young GI named Leon Rachman. They had two children, Dale Ellen and Alan Drew. Eventually, the family moved from New York to Southern California in 1956. Dora raised her children and volunteered as a community leader often; Girl Scout leader, PTA President, and County Election Board officer were just a few of the positions she held.

In addition to raising a family, Dora was a very creative and artistic person. A good cook, she also designed and sewed her own clothes, painted, sketched, and wrote poetry. But more importantly, she had a vivid imagination. In the early 60s, she began writing character-driven stories that combined human resilience, intrigue, and strong female voices.

Sometimes she would write late into the night, consumed by the characters she so vividly created. Although she did make some attempts to get published, she received lukewarm interest from the few publishers she contacted. Unfortunately, she was sidelined by ill health and passed away from cancer in 1972 at the age of 52, leaving behind a wealth of handwritten manuscripts, including several novels, short stories, and a children's book.

It took many years for me (her daughter) to be able to assemble these manuscripts into their final forms and find the right team to help me prepare them for publication. But at long last, they are ready to be presented to the public for everyone to enjoy. We hope that you find adventure, sadness, happiness, charm, and a sense of true joy in these works and share in the wonder and the spirit of humanity that my mother's characters bring to life.

DALE ELLEN LACASELLA